PRAISE F

MW01030711

"What instantly grabbed me was the camp. It transported me back to the summer camps I've visited. I could almost smell the outdoors, hear the birds singing and feel the water splash around me in the lake. You can tell the author has a great childhood memory of camp because you can't just make those feelings up. And how can you not fall in love with these characters? Everything in this book equals a hit. It's fun for the whole family and has lessons of family, God, love and friendship that can be learned by readers of all ages."

—SAMANTHA COVILLE OF SAMMYTHEBOOKWORM.COM,
REVIEWER FOR THE WORDSMITH JOURNAL MAGAZINE

"Admittedly, I have always been a fan of tween fiction...can't get enough of it. *Hear No Evil* didn't fail to keep me entertained. The book deals with bullying, having a handicap, pre-teen crushes and how God is with you during all the storms of life. Mom's reason for leaving him isn't revealed until the very end, leaving the reader in suspense through the entire novel."

—ANNETTE

BOOKS BY MARY HAMILTON

Taylor knew having his sister, Marissa, at camp would be a pain, but he never expected the pain to go so deep.

Taylor returns to camp with the goal of staying out of trouble long enough to earn his driver's license. Marissa believes in him and his dreams, but her mischievous spirit keeps landing *him* in trouble. When she falls for his snobbish cabin mate. Taylor is pulled into a war of words and pranks that escalates until it threatens to destroy every one of Taylor's dreams.

Steven Miller guards a dark secret.

Determined to honor his dad's memory, Steven recruits Dillon to help him train for a triathlon while attending camp for his last summer. When Dillon shows an interest in Claire after receiving sext messages from a girl back home, Steven feels compelled to protect Claire while keeping Dillon from falling into a familiar trap. But can Steven accomplish both without exposing his own shameful past?

E HEAR NO EVIL

RUSTIC KNOLL BIBLE CAMP
BOOK ONE

For Courtney Joel,
You were fearfully &
wonderfully made! Ps. 139:14
Believe it.
Mary L. Hamilton

MARY L. HAMILTON

To my LHGH girls
and every kid who feels rejected

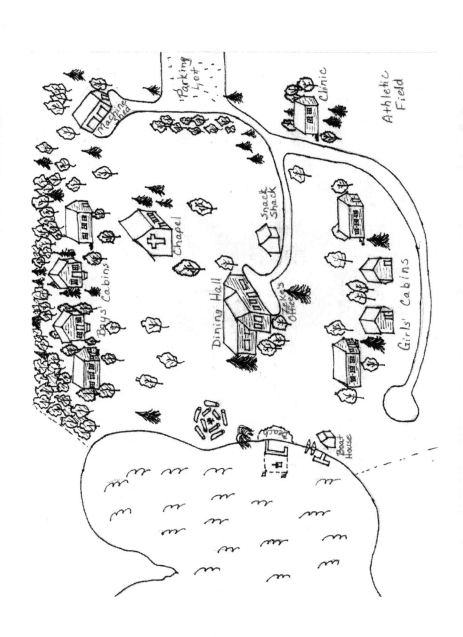

CHAPTER 1

The last time Mom chewed her lip like that was after Dad left. Brady McCaul shuddered. His memory of that day when he was seven years old was so clear, it might have happened just last week rather than six years ago.

He stole a glance at his mom as she sat behind the wheel of their old Taurus. Flecks of dried blood dotted her bottom lip from constant gnawing, just like in the weeks and months after Dad walked out on them. She hadn't said more than eight words since they left home in Chicago two hours ago. Several times she started to say something, but never quite got the words out. Something was bothering her, but it never did any good to ask. She'd give him a weak smile and start talking about the weather or school. *What could possibly be as bad as Dad leaving?*

Maybe some music would take his mind off the twinge in the pit of his stomach. He sighed and sank further into the

9

passenger's seat, propping his knees against the dashboard. He adjusted his earphones and bobbed his head to the beat of trumpet jazz by his one of his favorite artists. It didn't help, though. Even the music couldn't keep him from worrying about Mom. *Why would she chew her lip like that?*

After the first few dairy farms and cornfields, the scenery all looked the same and Brady became oblivious to it. They'd been following a pokey pickup truck loaded with bales of hay, doing at least ten miles under the speed limit. Mom accelerated and zoomed around, only to stomp on the brake and make a screeching right turn. An arrow-shaped sign on the corner read "Rustic Knoll Bible Camp."

Brady clutched the armrest with one hand and braced his other against the dashboard. The pickup's horn blared as it continued past them on the road they'd just left. Mom ducked her head, but her lips moved as she peeked at the rear view mirror.

He pulled out one ear bud. "What'd you say?"

"I said I'm sorry. I didn't mean to cut him off, but I couldn't see the sign until I got around him."

Brady twirled the earphone by its cord. "Was this Richard's idea? Me going to summer camp, I mean?" It still seemed weird, even after seven months, to call his stepdad by his first name. But calling him 'Dad' never felt right either.

Mom kept her focus on the road. "No, it was my decision." She accelerated again and they flew over the crest of a hill.

Brady pinched the earphone between his thumb and forefinger. "Richard doesn't like me any more than Dad did."

Mom teeth pinched her lower lip. "Give it time, honey. It's a big adjustment for all of us." She gave him a sideways glance, her eyes moist.

What is bothering her? He played with the button that raised and lowered the window. The sweet fragrance of fresh-cut hay lying in neat rows in the fields they passed tickled his nostrils. Hopefully, this place wasn't a boot camp or something. With a name like Rustic Knoll, he almost expected tents and outhouses.

A wooden sign with blue lettering and carved pine trees marked the camp's entrance. Gravel crunched under the tires as they pulled into the parking lot. He sneezed at the dust cloud that caught up with them as the car came to a stop. Before he opened the door, Mom's hand rested on his arm.

"I love you, Brady. I'm going to miss you."

"It's only for a week, Mom." She opened her mouth as if she were going to say something, but then clamped her lips shut and nodded. He unplugged his other ear and stuffed the mp3 player into the glove compartment. They weren't allowed to have electronic equipment at camp. Brady frowned as he got out of the car. Was there any chance Mom wouldn't embarrass him by getting all mushy when they said good-bye? He gathered his backpack, duffle bag, pillow, sleeping bag and trumpet case from the trunk.

"Got everything?" Mom closed her car door. "Here, let me carry something."

He handed over his pillow and sleeping bag then followed her past a welcome sign to a registration table shaded by a large oak. A few people waited in line ahead of them, so Brady dropped his duffle bag and set his trumpet case on the ground. He probably should have left the trumpet home, but if this place were as bad as he expected, he'd at least have one thing he could enjoy.

While the line inched forward, he checked out his surroundings. One low building sprawled in front of him, its wood siding stained deep reddish-brown. Another with a steep roof and cross-shaped window stood nearby. Beyond that, Brady glimpsed a cluster of smaller buildings, but nothing that looked like an outhouse. That seemed promising.

The woman behind them chatted with Mom, introducing herself as Mrs. Miller and the boy by her side as her son, Steven. He wore dark sunglasses and stood a few inches taller than Brady. One of his hands rested in the crook of his mom's elbow. The other he thrust out in front of him.

"Nice to meet you." He spoke the words but looked straight ahead.

Brady wasn't sure the kid was speaking to him, but Mom was talking to Mrs. Miller and he was the only one left in their little group. He reached out and shook Steven's hand.

"You, too." As soon as he spoke, Steven turned in his direction. *He's blind.*

"Where are you from?" Steven asked.

"Chicago."

"Same here! What part?"

"The northwest side." Brady didn't want to give some strange kid his whole life story. He looked to Mom to help him out, but her gaze darted between the people in line, the ground, and the registration table. Everywhere but him. Was she angry? She didn't exactly act as if she were mad at him. Why couldn't she just come out and tell him what was wrong?

Thankfully, the woman at the check-in table motioned them forward, and Brady scooted his duffle bag and trumpet case ahead until he stood in front of her.

"Welcome to Rustic Knoll. I'm Nurse Willie." She reached across the table. "Do you have your health form?" A light blue medical scrub top accented her dark skin. Wiry white curls puffed out from beneath the rim of her bucket hat, reminding Brady of small clouds. The fishing lures adorning her hat looked crazy, but cool at the same time, and they made faint tinkling sounds whenever her head moved.

Brady shrugged out of his backpack and dug around inside for his health form. "It's in here somewhere."

While he rifled through the compartments, Nurse Willie pointed out a spot on her hat to the younger man seated beside her.

"New lure?" he asked.

"Yep. Tried it out this weekend. Couldn't even snag a clump of seaweed. Adds a nice touch of color though, don't you think?"

"It's you, Willie," he chuckled. "Definitely you."

Brady checked his pockets and dug through his backpack again. "I know I put it in here."

Mom started to unzip his duffle bag. "You didn't leave it at home, did you?"

"Nope. Found it." Brady held up a wrinkled health form.

Nurse Willie took it from him and looked it over. The younger man beside her leaned close and squinted at the top of the paper, then checked a list in front of him. He looked older than a high schooler, but not really grown up yet. He drew a line with his yellow highlighter, then raised his head and smiled.

"Brady McCaul? All right! You're in my cabin this week. I'm your counselor, Matt Carpenter." He held up his hand for a high-five.

Brady met his hand and grinned back at Mom. His counselor seemed promising, at least.

Matt pointed off to his left. "We're in Oaks Cabin, on the other side of the chapel. You're free until supper. Meet me in the cabin a little before six and we'll all go eat together."

Brady gathered up his belongings and headed in the direction Matt had pointed. Mom followed, lagging behind. They hadn't gone far when she called him to stop. He turned to find her hugging his pillow and sleeping bag the way his little cousin held her teddy bear when she was crying. "What's wrong?"

She shook the hair from her face. "There's something I need to tell you. I've been putting it off, trying to think of the best way to say it, but..." She pressed her lips together and her chin quivered.

"I know something's wrong. What is it?" Brady stood waiting, but she remained silent, biting her lip. "Mom. Just say it."

She inhaled deeply as if to push the words out. They rushed from her mouth. "You can't come home at the end of the week. Your dad is picking you up. You'll be living with him now."

Brady's jaw dropped. "What? Whose idea was that? Richard's?"

Mom closed her eyes, swallowed hard and rolled her lips in. "No. It's my decision."

"Mom." Brady stretched the word into two syllables. People turned to look at them, and he lowered his voice. "Why?"

"You're growing up." She tried to smile, but her lips trembled too much. "You're almost fourteen...and...you need your dad."

Brady's legs threatened to give out on him. He shook his head. "I need a dad who cares about me more than his job. Dad doesn't even bother to send me a birthday card unless you remind him."

Mom straightened her back and shoulders, and she took

on a firm tone. "Honey, I can't explain it, but you need to be with your dad right now."

His dropped his duffle bag and it thudded on the ground. "I don't want to live with Dad. I'd never see my friends anymore. I'd have to change schools. Why can't I stay with you?"

"I told you why..."

"But in the car you told me to give Richard time. You said it's an adjustment."

Mom sighed and shook her head. "Don't argue with me. You're only making this harder."

"Me?" He brought his hands to his chest then flung his arms out to the side. "I'm not making it harder. You're the one who came up with this dumb idea. You get to go back home. To Richard." The last two words came out as a sneer.

"Stop it!" Mom's eyes narrowed. "You may not talk like that to me."

Brady wasn't finished. "You're just like Dad. You don't care about me either."

"That's enough!" She threw the sleeping bag and pillow to the ground, then crossed her arms and hugged her shoulders. She looked like she was trying to warm herself. "I don't want you living with me anymore, Brady. This is not up for discussion. Your father will pick you up on Saturday."

She turned on her heel and marched to the parking lot where she slumped against the car. Her hand fumbled with the keys and brushed across her eyes more than once before she got the door open. She put one foot in the car, then stopped and looked his way.

Come back, Mom. Please, come back and tell me it was all a mistake.

She sat in the car. Did he hear the rumble of the engine

15

coming to life, or was it his imagination? Either way, the scene was all too real. Gravel sprayed as Mom spun the car around and drove away without even a backhand wave. It was eerily familiar, except the last time, he was seven years old, hiding in his room with a pillow over his head to keep out the angry voices. A door slammed, and everything went silent. He threw back the pillow and heard Mom crying, then jumped off the bed and ran to the window to watch his dad drive away. Dad never returned Brady's wave. Never returned, period.

Breathe. His throat hurt from swallowing back tears, and he bit his tongue until he tasted blood. Dipping his head, he clamped his eyes shut against the curious stares. His cheeks and the tips of his ears burned. Opening his eyes to the duffle bag at his feet, he reared his foot back, then shot it forward to slam into the bag. The zipper split, and underwear, shorts and t-shirts belched from the overstuffed bag onto the ground. He let go a shaky breath then squatted to gather up his clothes.

Matt appeared beside him. "Here, let me help you with that." He grabbed a handful of underwear and stuffed it back in the bag.

Brady rubbed away a tear that dripped onto his hand before Matt could see it. "I'll do it."

Matt moved close and whispered, "I want to help. I figure you probably feel like this bag right now. Kicked in the gut, split open, all your insides falling out?"

Brady pressed his lips into a hard line. He rubbed his eyes with the heel of his hand.

"Don't worry. We'll get you outta here in a second." Matt looked around. "Hey, Steven. Come here a minute."

Steven and his mother were just leaving the check-in table. They came and stood beside Matt as he introduced the boys.

"Steven Miller, meet Brady McCaul. You're both in my cabin."

Steven nodded toward Matt. "We already met in line. I take it this is your first time at Rustic Knoll?"

Brady nodded.

"Speak up," Matt said. "He can't see you nod."

"Yeah." Brady cleared his throat. "Yeah, it is." The pitying look in Mrs. Miller's eyes told him she'd heard everything. He looked away, embarrassed.

Matt spoke to both Steven and his mom. "We need some help getting Brady to the cabin. The zipper on his duffle bag broke. Do you have an extra hand?"

Steven shifted his sleeping bag from his hand to underneath his arm and accepted the trumpet case from Matt. "Musical instrument?"

Brady nodded. *Oh yeah, say things out loud.* "It's a trumpet."

"You must be good."

"How would you know that?" Brady scrunched his eyebrows together as he packed his sleeping bag and pillow under one arm.

"Just a guess. Sometimes kids bring guitars to camp but not horns. Bringing a horn to camp says you love playing it, and people who love playing something are usually good at it."

Brady shrugged. "I guess."

Mrs. Miller tugged at her son's shirt collar to straighten it. "Steven, why don't we say good-bye here so you can show Brady to the cabin?"

"What about my suitcase?" Steven asked.

"Here, let's do this." Matt wrapped the duffle bag's strap around it to keep it closed then slid it down around the suitcase's pull-out handle. "There. Now one of you can pull

17

it."

Brady busied himself with his gear while Steven and his mom hugged and said their good-byes. His chest ached with envy at the way she rubbed Steven's back while they embraced. Mom used to rub his back every night. The night Dad left, she'd found him crying in bed; she'd stayed and rubbed his back until he fell asleep. It grew into a routine that morphed into a back scratch as he got older.

A lot had changed lately. Mom rarely came to his room to say good night anymore. He was pretty certain Dad would never bother to scratch his back.

Mrs. Miller positioned Steven's hand on Brady's elbow, squeezed both boys' shoulders and said, "You're all set. Off to the cabin with you."

Brady hesitated. "Isn't it kind of hard to find your way around camp when you're…"

"Blind? Trust me. I've been coming here since I was little. I prob'ly know this place better than most of the people who work here."

Brady took a few cautious steps.

"Just walk normal," Steven said, "but let me know if they've rearranged the furniture."

"Furniture?"

"Warn me if I need to step up, over, around, or down."

Brady nodded, then remembered to say okay. He started toward the cabin that would be his new home, at least for the next six days. After that? If he wanted to live with Mom, he'd have to figure out why she'd kicked him out. Maybe then, he'd be able to change her mind. But one thing was certain; he would not be living with Dad.

CHAPTER 2

Steven chattered all the way to the cabin. Something about boat races and a girl named Claire. Mom's words played over and over in Brady's head. What had he done that was so awful she didn't want him living with her anymore?

Four squat buildings nestled among trees at the edge of some woods. Brady guessed which one was Oaks Cabin from the trees surrounding it. Two concrete steps led up to a screen door that screeched when he opened it. He stopped inside to let his eyes adjust to the dark interior.

"What's wrong?" Steven's fingers tightened slightly on Brady's arm.

"Nothing. I just can't see anything until my eyes adjust."

Steven laughed. "I don't have that problem. Follow me." He let go of Brady's arm and took measured steps across the room.

Brady followed. The outlines of several couches took

shape against the walls of the common room.

"The bathroom and showers are over there." Steven pointed to the left, then rapped his knuckles on a closed door as they passed it. "Counselor's room, where Matt sleeps." He moved through a wide doorway, his arm stretched out ahead of him until his hand touched a bunk bed. "Is this one taken?"

Three boys looked up from their huddle over a car magazine on the lower bed. The boy in the middle tossed the hair from his eyes and grimaced.

"Pull your shades off and maybe you could see us sitting here," he said.

"Is that all it takes?" Steven whipped his glasses off, revealing milky-looking eyes as he turned his head in one direction, then another. He clicked his tongue. "Nope, not that easy." The other two boys elbowed the one who spoke, and whispers hissed between them.

"Come on." Brady pulled Steven down the row past three other bunk beds to two empty ones on the end. "You want top or bottom?"

"I'm better off on the bottom. Where do you want your trumpet?"

One of the three teens looked up. "You brought a trumpet?"

The first kid blew through his lips and muttered loud enough for everyone to hear. "Loser."

Steven felt for the bottom bunk and sat on it. "He's not a loser. Wait 'til you hear him. Play something, Brady."

"I–I don't really feel like playing right now." He tried to take the trumpet case, but Steven pulled it onto his lap and opened the clasps.

"Come on," Steven begged. "Just a little? Play something. Anything."

A half-frown tugged at Brady's mouth.

One boy turned away from the magazine. "Go ahead. Play something."

With a sigh, Brady picked up the horn, slid the mouthpiece into place and licked his lips. After running through some basic scales, he began to improvise. Soon, the joy of the music took over. Inhaling a deep breath, he launched into a tune the boys recognized. Finally, he ended his performance by playing "Amazing Grace" in three different musical styles. By the time he finished, two of the three boys had turned away from the magazine and joined Steven's applause.

The first kid flipped a page with an exaggerated yawn. "I've heard better."

"Jealous, Taylor?" His friend gave the boy called Taylor a knowing grin.

"Shut up, Chris." Taylor scowled and pointed to the magazine. "Nick, look at this."

Chris moved over to Steven's bunk and nodded toward Taylor. "Don't let him get to you. That was really good. Play some more?"

"Maybe later." Brady put the horn away and closed the case. The open cabinets for hanging clothing offered nothing in the way of safekeeping. He slid it under Steven's bed then shoved his backpack and duffle bag along the sides to hide it from casual view. Later, he'd ask Matt about locking it up.

Brady nudged Steven's shoulder. "Let's get out of here."

They stopped on the front steps, and Steven drew a verbal map of the camp's grounds. "The lake is downhill from here. Swimming and boating are over that way." He pointed ahead and to the left. "Zeke's office and the dining hall are back where we came from. The girls' cabins are on the other side of the dining hall. Rec is over in that area too."

"Who is Zeke? And what's wreck? It sounds like a car wreck."

Steven grinned. "Zeke is the camp director. You'll meet him tonight. His real name is David Zacharias. Reverend Zacharias. Rec is short for recreation: baseball, tennis, basketball. I don't usually hang around the Rec area, for obvious reasons. But if you want to see it…"

"No, let's go see the lake." Brady winced. Steven couldn't see the lake or anything else. He'd have to be more careful about the words he used.

The trees soon thinned out, giving way to a grassy hillside that descended to the beach. A light breeze carried the unique scent of sand and water. Sunlight glittered on the lake like the little white Christmas lights Mom put on their shrubs at home. Speedboats zoomed in every direction, some pulling water-skiers.

A silvery aluminum pier enclosed three sides of a swimming area where a game of water tag was going on. The swimmers' shouts and laughter carried up to where Brady stood. Beyond the pier, a pontoon raft with a diving board floated in place. Ropes and buoys marked the boundaries of the deep-water area.

"Do you swim, Brady?"

"I know how, but that's about it." A contest out on the raft caught Brady's attention. A group of boys competed for the biggest splash off the diving board. He recalled launching himself from the edge of the pool when he was three or four, his body drawn into a ball. The splashes he made couldn't have been anything like the ones these boys were making, but Mom always acted as if they were gigantic.

Steven interrupted his daydream. "I bet Claire's down

there somewhere. She loves the water."

"There's a bunch of girls sunbathing. What does she look like?" Brady winced again. "Um...I mean...sorry."

Steven laughed. "Don't worry. It's cool when people forget I'm different. Anyway, Claire wouldn't be lying around on the beach. She'd be out in the water."

Just then, a distant voice called, "Steven!"

"That's her." Steven nodded once. "Do you see her? Where is she?"

Brady's gaze swept the beach and swimming area then moved over to the boat dock. The voice rang out again, and he spotted two girls in a canoe nearing the dock. One waved an arm in the air, as if Steven could see her.

"She's down by the boats. You want to go see...I mean, go down there?"

Steven was already pulling in that direction. Brady warned him when they reached the steps leading down to the boat dock.

Steven smiled. "I know. There's seven, and they're kind of wide from front to back."

"How do you know that?"

"I've done these steps every year since I was five. That's ten years in a row."

The wooden boat dock jutted into the water like a T, with a small ski boat tethered to one side. To the right, six canoes lay beached on the sand. Claire met them at the bottom step, giving Steven an awkward hug in her life vest. She stood slightly taller than him with an athletic build and blonde hair in a boyish cut. She pulled off her life jacket and tossed it to her friend who was returning their gear to the boathouse.

"Dillon's back this year," Claire said, "but his leg's in a cast."

Steven laughed. "Really? Mighty Dillon, the super jock, with a cast on his leg?"

"No kidding. Of course, he's bragging about how he broke it." Claire looked from Steven to Brady. "Hi. I'm Claire. That's Hayley."

Brady stuttered. "Uh, hi. I'm Brady." Girls as cute as Claire usually acted like he was invisible. He blamed it on his red hair and freckles.

"Did you come to camp with Steven?" Claire asked. Brady shook his head.

"We're in the same cabin," Steven explained. "What are you up to?"

"We were just going to swim. Want to come?"

"Not unless Brady wants to. We'd have to go back to the cabin and change."

Claire's smile drooped and the dimples in her cheeks disappeared. "You'll be sorry."

"Maybe tomorrow," Brady offered. He might actually start to like swimming.

Her smile perked up again. "All right then. Come on, Hayley. Let's go."The girls ran off to the beach, and Steven made a suggestion.

"Since we're here, let's take out a canoe."

"I've never been in one before."

"It's not hard. I'll steer. You just paddle and tell me if we need to go right or left. Go get us some life jackets and paddles."

The boat manager provided the necessary equipment and introduced himself as Ryan, the counselor in Spruce cabin next door to Oaks. Brady handed a life jacket to Steven and pulled the other orange vest over his head. He tied the top lashes and buckled the strap around his waist, then led Steven to a canoe.

Ryan joined them, eyeing Steven.

"You sure you're okay taking one of these out?"

Brady would've readily agreed to stay on shore, but Steven spoke up.

"We're fine. Zeke can tell you I've done this many times." He snapped the buckle on his vest. "Blow your whistle if you don't like what you see and we'll come back."

"All right." Ryan sounded unconvinced. "Wait. How'd you know I have a whistle?"

Steven sighed. "I told you I've done this before. Lifeguards and boat guys all have whistles. Now, would you mind showing Brady how to paddle?"

Minutes later, in the nose of the canoe, Brady held tight to the sides while Steven's paddle swished through the water behind him. The canoe skimmed along so smoothly, he gradually loosened his grip on the gunwales. He took up his paddle, gripping it the way Ryan had showed him, and dipped it into the water. It dragged as the canoe moved forward. He pulled the paddle up to try again, but the canoe tipped to the right. He yelped, grabbed for the gunwales and nearly dropped the paddle in the lake.

"What happened? You okay?" Steven's voice held concern.

Brady swallowed. "I thought we were tipping over."

"Sorry, I just shifted positions. The boat won't sink, even if we do go over, but it's really not as tippy as it feels. Hang on. I'll show you."

Brady clung to the sides while Steven rocked the boat, gently at first, gradually building up to a point where Brady held his breath in case he landed in the water.

Ryan's whistle blast ended the experiment. "What are you doing?"

Steven called back. "Just getting him used to the motion. That's all. We're done." He dropped his voice to talk to Brady. "See? It tips pretty far without going over."

Brady's pulse returned to normal, and he stuck his paddle in the water again, pulling back hard. The paddle hit the side of the canoe, so he switched to the other side and tried again. That was even more awkward than the other way.

Steven coached him. "It's okay to switch sides whenever your arms get tired, but it's better if we work together. Try paddling when I say stroke. Ready? Stroke. Stroke. Stroke."

They glided into deeper water. It looked like it might be a mile or more to the other side of the lake. The shore swept around them in the wide arc of a natural bay. Ryan had warned them not to go past an imaginary line across the bay's opening. But it was tempting to go farther. A blue and white sailboat slid across the open lake as if pulled along on an unseen string.

Houses occupied the shoreline on both sides of Rustic Knoll, some newer and more elaborate than others. Here and there, a dilapidated boathouse sat next to a newer aluminum dock where motorboats, pontoons, jet skis, and even a paddleboat were tied up.

The canoe rocked over several speedboat wakes, and Brady enjoyed the feel of rolling with the waves. Before long, though, his arms grew heavy, like they were dragging fifty-pound weights.

"I need to stop a minute. My arms are about to fall off."

Steven stopped paddling. "Want to have some fun?"

"Not if it means you'll tip us over."

Steven laughed. "I wouldn't do that to you. My dad tipped me over on purpose one of the first times he took me out here."

Brady half turned and spoke over his shoulder. "Why'd he

do that?"

"Dad didn't believe in making things easy for me. He made me do lots of stuff that seemed pointless at the time."

"Like what?"

"Counting steps, for one thing. Every time we came up here, Dad had me count how many steps from the bunk to the bathroom, cabin to the dining hall, cabin to the beach. Everywhere we went, he had me memorizing how to orient myself at one place to get somewhere else. He said it would teach me confidence."

Brady straddled his seat so he could see Steven.

"I hated it." Steven fiddled with the paddle lying across his knees. "All that counting and planning and thinking. It seemed so stupid at the time. But since Dad died last year, I appreciate what he did for me. He forced me to be independent." Steven paused, then inhaled deeply and sat up straight. "That's why he tipped the canoe over. He always tried to prepare me for the worst thing that could possibly happen so I'd know how to handle unexpected trouble."

Brady pulled his other leg around and faced Steven. "How did you handle it?"

"Not very well." Steven laughed. "One minute I'm sitting in the canoe and the next I'm in the lake, trying to breathe. I wanted to scream or cry, but all I could do was gulp water."

"He didn't even warn you?"

"Nope. You should've heard my mom when she found out about it. But when we got back, Dad said he did it that way because I can't see what's coming and he wanted me to be able to manage surprises." Steven shrugged. "I survived, and I know what to do if it happens again."

Brady played with the strap on his vest. "Sounds like he was pretty tough on you."

"Sometimes he was, but we had fun too." Steven sat quietly for several moments. "I sure miss him." He picked up his paddle and dragged it through the water.

Brady couldn't say he missed his dad. Broken promises and neglect had a way of killing any warm memories. Besides, seeing his mom cry had scared him worse than his dad leaving. The ache in his chest deepened.

In silence, Brady swung around to face the front and dug his paddle into the water. Again. And again.

"Everything okay, Brady?"

"Yeah." I hate my dad. And I hate Mom, too, for leaving me.

"You sure?"

"I'm fine."

Hate my life.

"If I said something wrong…"

"I said I'm fine. Can we go back now?"

The canoe began to swing around.

"Remember, you're the navigator," Steven said. "Tell me where you want to go."

Home. I want to go home.

CHAPTER 3

Hours later, Brady stepped sideways into the back row of the chapel for evening worship. Steven followed, grasping his elbow, but Claire hung back in the aisle.

"I don't want to sit way back here. Come on, let's go up front." She grabbed Steven's hand and led him up the center aisle to the third row on the left.

Brady followed. *What am I? A little brother tagging along on a date?* Not that Steven or Claire ever made him feel unwelcome. In fact, having Claire around relieved him of guide dog status. What he didn't like was when she got a little bossy. Like now. She and Steven had such an easy way with each other. Did their friendship go deeper than summer camp buddies? Probably not after the way she pulled away from Steven's grasp even before they sat down.

A damp, musty odor tickled Brady's nose and he sneezed. Fans hung from the vaulted ceiling, their swirling blades mixing the day's accumulated heat with cooler evening air sucked in through the open windows. Fading sunlight filtered through the blue cross-shaped window at the front, bathing a low stage in soft colored shadows.

Ryan tinkered with a drum set on the stage while other counselors tuned guitars and checked microphones. At the start of the first song, all the kids got to their feet. Matt slipped in beside Brady and started clapping and singing along with the music. The song was unfamiliar to Brady, but before long his fingers were following the beat, tapping on the pew in front of him. Several lively songs followed before the band turned the stage over to Zeke, and everyone sat down.

Steven had introduced him to Zeke at supper, but now Brady studied the man setting an oversized pad of drawing paper up on an easel. His squat stature, white hair and matching mustache made him look more like one of Santa's elves than a camp director.

Zeke removed the lid from a thin box and selected a piece of artist's chalk, the kind Brady's art teacher called pastels. He sketched several black streaks on the paper then held his hand in the air. "Raise your hand if you know me." Steven and Claire raised their hands, along with most of the other campers.

Zeke cocked an eyebrow, then drew a few more black streaks. "Does anyone here know Abraham Lincoln?" This time, Brady raised his hand with the others.

"You do?" Both of Zeke's eyebrows shot up this time. "What about George Washington?" He stepped back at the enthusiastic response and covered his heart with his hand. His head moved back and forth and his white brows knit together in a puzzled expression. He added a few more black strokes before choosing a new color.

Steven leaned over and whispered to Brady. "What's he drawing?"

"I can't tell yet. Just some black streaks."

Zeke colored in a few areas while he spoke. "You know, it's one thing to know who someone is. When I finish this drawing, every one of you will recognize him." He waved his hand over the audience, a piece of bright red chalk clenched in his fingers. "You'll know his name. You'll know what he does, where he lives. But will you really know him?"

He drew in more details. "Think about your best friend. Do you know what makes her laugh? Or cry? What makes him angry? Do you know her favorite color or food? Does he root for the Cubs or the Brewers? Can you recognize her voice? If he called your name in the school cafeteria, would you know who it was without looking?"

"It's the President!" Brady tried to keep his voice down. "Wow! It looks just like him."

Zeke put the finishing touches on his drawing and dropped the chalk back in the box. He rubbed his fingers on a towel. "Now, do you know this man?"

Several campers shouted out his name.

Zeke spoke to a girl on the front row. "Do you know what makes him laugh?" He pointed to other campers and asked, "What TV shows does he like to watch? What's his favorite ice cream flavor? Without looking, would you know his voice if he called your name?"

Zeke picked up a Bible and strolled down the aisle. "You see, there's a difference between knowing who someone is and knowing them personally. People make that mistake with God. They may know a lot about Him, but they haven't spent time getting to know Him. They can't recognize His voice. He could scream in their ear and they'd never hear it."

Brady studied the chalk portrait. He'd always thought you got to know God by going to church. His family went when he was little, but it hadn't done much good. His dad still left; his parents still divorced. He and his mom quit going to church after the divorce. Maybe he only knew *about* God, like Zeke said. He wouldn't recognize God's voice. But then, God would never call his name anyway.

***

Darkness pressed in on Brady when he left the chapel. Nighttime never looked this black at home. Matt flicked on his flashlight and let it play over the ground in front of them.

Brady fell into step beside Matt. "Thanks. I left my flashlight in the cabin."

"Yeah, so did I." Steven's fingers held Brady's elbow with a light touch.

Why would Steven have a flashlight? Brady caught Matt's puzzled look and shrugged.

Steven squeezed his arm. "That's a joke. You're supposed to laugh."

"Oh!" Matt chuckled. "I thought maybe you had some fancy new flashlight that beeped when something was in your way." They all laughed as they walked toward the cabin. Brady kept a close watch on the ground for anything that might trip Steven.

"So how's camp going for you guys so far?" Matt asked.

Brady nudged Steven sideways, skirting an old stump. "It's okay."

"Just wait 'til tomorrow." Steven smacked his lips. "It gets better, starting with Janie's pancakes and sausage for breakfast."

Matt laughed. "You've been coming here way too long if you know the menu that well. Either that or Janie's in a serious rut."

"Who's Janie?" Brady asked.

Matt flicked the flashlight beam back and forth. "Janie Rodriguez is Rustic Knoll's head cook and substitute mom. You'll see her around the buffet lines at meals. She even takes special requests if you compliment her cooking."

They reached the cabin where raucous voices erupted from within. At the top of the steps, Matt held the door open, motioning Brady and Steven inside. Something whizzed past Brady's head.

"Ouch!" Steven rubbed his cheek. "What was that?"

A yellow peanut M&M fell at their feet. Another one smacked against the doorframe. Matt pushed past them and stalked through the common room, stopping in the doorway to the bunkroom.

"Whoever threw those better get rid of them now! If I see 'em, they're mine."

A hurried rustling sounded, and a voice apologized. "I didn't mean to hit you. Honest."

"You hit Steven, not me. Make sure you pick up every piece of candy that's on the floor if you don't want ants crawling on you in your sleep."

Matt waved Brady and Steven in. Damp swim trunks lay in a puddle of water on the floor. T-shirts and beach towels were flung over the ends of beds. Sleeping bags, once positioned neatly on the bunks, now dangled over the sides. Open suitcases with contents in disarray littered the aisle.

"Get these out of the way so no one trips over them." Matt kicked one of the suitcases under a bed and waited until the rest were cleared from the path. Brady led Steven to their bunks.

"You have fifteen minutes to get ready for bed. Then I

want everyone out here." Matt pointed to the common room. "Fifteen minutes."

Brady dragged his duffle bag from under the bed, relieved to see his trumpet case where he'd left it. He and Steven got ready for bed and brushed their teeth before finding seats on a couch in the common room. Taylor wandered in with Nick and Chris, and claimed an entire couch for himself. He stretched his legs the length of it, kicking Nick off when he tried to squeeze in on the end. Chris grabbed a cushion from another chair, threw it on the floor, and sat on it.

When everyone had assembled, Matt made his way around the room, reviewing the boys' names and asking each one a few questions. He stopped in front of Brady, held the tip of his thumb to his lips and wiggled his fingers up and down. "I hear you brought a trumpet. Can you play?"

Brady gulped. "Now?"

Matt grinned. "No, I mean, are you any good?"

Brady shrugged, hoping it would discourage any further attention.

Steven didn't let it pass. "You should hear him."

"He is pretty awesome." Nick nodded, but said no more when Taylor slapped his shoulder.

Chris paid no attention to Taylor's scowl. "Have him play something."

"A fan club already." Matt looked impressed. "Know any lullabies that'll put these animals to sleep?"

"'Amazing Grace,'" Steven blurted out. "Seriously, you should hear the way he plays it."

Would he never shut up?

Chris agreed with Steven, and Matt looked at Brady.

"Will you play it for us tonight when we turn the lights out?"

Brady drew air through his nostrils before agreeing. He should have left the trumpet at home. No, better to have it with him, since he may not have a home anymore. *Was Mom really as serious as she sounded?*

She's changed. Frozen pizzas and popcorn used to mark Friday nights after Dad left. He and Mom would camp out in the living room and watch a rented movie, sometimes falling asleep right there on the floor. If only he could still talk to her like he did during their Friday night specials. *When did we stop doing that? And why? Was it because I got older? Or because she met Richard?*

Matt's voice cut into his thoughts. "Be out here with your trumpet in about ten minutes, okay?"

Brady nodded. Not one word Matt said had gone into his ears after he agreed to play. He guided Steven back to their bunks and waited while his friend unzipped his sleeping bag and pulled back the top. Inside was a folded bed sheet. Smart idea. The cabin held in the day's heat like a dry sauna. A cool sheet sounded so much better than a heavy sleeping bag. As soon as Steven got into bed, Brady reached underneath and pulled out his trumpet case.

"Are you going to play it the way you did this afternoon?"

Brady lifted his trumpet and shut the case. "No. I think I'll just play it straight."

"You should play it for the talent show at the end of the week."

Brady ignored that suggestion. "I need to see about locking this up." With the horn in one hand and the case in the other, he went to Matt's open door.

"Can I lock this up somewhere?"

Matt pointed to an empty corner. "You can leave it here if you want. I lock the room whenever I leave. But if you want to play it when I'm not here, you'll have to find me to get the key."

Brady pressed his lips together. "Let's try it." He set the case just inside the door and went out to the common room to wait.

Matt herded stragglers out of the bathroom and into their bunks. Finally, amid much chatter and noise, Matt cut the lights off in the bunkroom. He leaned against the door jam, framed by the light from his room, and gave the signal to begin playing.

Brady licked his lips and raised the trumpet. The soothing notes of the familiar song flowed out in long, restful tones. When the last one died away, the silence in the bunkroom surprised him, as did the sudden applause from Spruce cabin next door.

"I think your fan club just exploded." Matt pushed away from the doorframe, placed his hands on Brady's shoulders and looked him in the eye. "That was really good. You've got talent. A real gift. You are awesome." Matt squeezed his shoulders and gave him a pat on the back.

Brady laid his horn in the case and headed back to his bunk.

"Loser." The whisper followed him, but other voices answered back.

"Shut up, Taylor."

He climbed onto his bunk, laid his head on the pillow and stared at the dark ceiling. Was his talent really that unusual?

You. Are. Awesome. The words echoed inside his head, each one emphasized as if Matt really meant it.

If I'm so awesome, why doesn't Mom want me anymore? Why did Dad leave?

Loser.

CHAPTER 4

Brady struggled to open one eye when someone prodded him.

"Wake up. It's time for breakfast." Steven joggled his shoulder. "If you want a shower, you better get in there now before everyone else gets up." He pulled a towel from around his neck and rubbed it over his wet hair.

Brady yawned and stretched. He'd lain awake last night long after the light in Matt's room went out and the other boys' whispers turned to soft snores. Mom's parting words kept echoing in his head. "I don't want you living with me anymore." *I don't want you.* He'd pulled the pillow over his ears, hoping to shut out the ugly words. It worked for a time, but during the night, he awoke and listened to their echoes for hours before finally falling asleep again. He couldn't have slept more than thirty minutes before Steven woke him.

He climbed down from his bunk. He wouldn't bother changing from the shorts and t-shirt he'd slept in. They were

37

wrinkled, but he wasn't awake enough to think about finding his shower stuff. He'd have time to shower and change after breakfast.

"I guess I'm ready." He yawned once again, ran his fingers through his hair and took a good look at Steven.

His friend's dark blond hair lay in place across his head, parted smartly on the left. Steven's striped pullover shirt looked crisp, as if he'd just pulled it from an ironing board. It was tucked into his shorts, which were also unwrinkled and belted at the waist. Somehow, he managed to avoid the geeky look that plagued other kids who dressed that way.

How does he do that when he can't even see himself in a mirror?

Other boys were stirring by the time they left the cabin. The sun was high enough to peek through the trees, dappling the ground with light as they headed for the dining hall. Yesterday's heat still clung to the air.

Steven inhaled. "Mmmm. Smell those pancakes? Trust me. They're worth getting up for." He slowed as they neared the Snack Shack. "Take a look at the activities board and tell me what Rec team I'm on."

Brady moved around to the Shack's side where a glass-covered announcement board was mounted on the outer wall. He skimmed over the lists of Rec teams. "You're on the red team. Hey, so am I!"

"Yes! Anyone else on our team? What are we playing today?"

Brady scanned the list again, relieved at not seeing Taylor's name. "Looks like Claire and Chris are with us. I hope they're good at softball 'cause that's what we're doing. I hate softball."

Steven shook his head. "I'm not crazy about it either. Not

since I got hit by a ball."

In the dining hall, Brady slid a tray along the buffet line. He loaded Steven's plate then piled a stack of pancakes on his own, along with a generous helping of sausages.

"Here's some hot syrup for you boys." A plump, older woman slid a pan of steaming pancake syrup into the buffet. Her eyes lit when she saw Steven. "How come you didn't let me know you were here?" She waddled around the end of the buffet, pulling off her sanitary serving gloves, and gave him a hug.

A wide smile creased Steven's face. "Hi, Janie. I missed you at supper last night. I've been bragging to Brady here about your pancakes."

She reached to shake his hand. "Hello, Brady. It's nice to meet you. I'm Janie Rodriguez."

"You too, Mrs. Rodriguez." It came out as a mumble. He still wasn't totally awake.

"Call me Janie." She tilted her head sideways to look at him. "Such pretty red hair. I think I'm jealous." She winked and returned to her side of the buffet.

Pretty?

"Well, Steven, what can I cook for you this week?" She pulled her serving gloves back on and waited for an answer.

Steven struck a pose that looked like he was deep in thought. "How about some sloppy joes, with brownies for dessert? And can we make it a picnic?"

"Anything for you, Steven. Which night would you like that?"

"Tomorrow night?"

"Done."

Steven laughed. "Thanks, Janie. See you later."

Brady led the way to a table. "Was she serious? Did you

really just decide what we're having for supper tomorrow?"

Steven laughed again. "No, it's a joke. We do this every year. Tuesday night is always picnic night with sloppy joes and brownies." He sat down and arranged his plate, utensils and glass just so, then bowed his head.

Brady stared at his plate. Steven had done the same thing at supper last night. Was he expected to pray too or was it okay to go ahead and eat? Fifteen minutes ago, food was the last thing on his mind, but now his stomach demanded breakfast. Still, it seemed rude to start eating while someone next to him was praying. He waited for Steven's head to come up, then stabbed a sausage and devoured it.

By the time he licked the last drop of syrup from his fork, the dining hall had filled up. Some of the boys from the cabin joined them at the table. Matt claimed the last empty spot.

"G'morning, men."

Only Steven answered with any enthusiasm. Brady pushed his tray back, crossed his arms on the table and laid his head down on top. He needed sleep. But a string of curse words from the table behind him brought his head up with a jerk.

Matt jumped to his feet. All eyes turned to the offending table where Taylor sat. The boys around him looked wide-eyed at Matt, lips clamped tight. Taylor turned around and clapped a hand over his mouth.

"Oops, I'm sorry. Really, I am. I know I'm not supposed to cuss here. I didn't mean to. Honest. Sorry."

A tight smile formed on Matt's lips, but his voice sounded casual. "No, no. Go right ahead. You can curse all you want."

Taylor's eyes narrowed, his brows forming a V. He looked at his friends around the table and then back at Matt. "Really?"

"Yeah, you can curse all you want. But you have to use

your own name. The other one's already taken and the owner doesn't appreciate it being used like that." He held Taylor's gaze until the boy turned away, bright pink creeping up his neck and face.

Brady snickered as Matt took his seat again. Uneasy laughter rippled from Taylor's table, while several boys at his own table quietly applauded. Steven raised his hand for a high five, and Matt reached over to slap it. Brady grinned and laid his head back down on the table.

"So, is everyone up for a full day today? Get enough sleep last night?" Matt's fork sliced through his pancakes.

"I did." Steven's cheerfulness contrasted with a variety of complaints from the other boys.

Brady moaned. "If we didn't have to get up at dawn for breakfast."

"Dawn?" Matt swallowed a large bite. "Around here, the sun's up a good two hours before you rolled out of bed." He stuffed a couple sausages in his mouth and tried to talk around them. "Did you guys check your Rec team? You know what you're doing today?"

Steven answered first. "Playing softball."

Matt stopped chewing and dropped his fork. It clattered against his plate. "Don't tell me you play ball, too."

"No way." Steven shook his head. "I used to cheer my team from the sidelines until I got hit by a foul ball. Now Zeke finds something else for me. I need to let him know and find out what he wants me to do."

"I'll take care of that for you. Are you both on the same team?" Matt picked up his fork and pointed it at Steven and Brady.

Brady nodded without lifting his head. He stifled a yawn.

Matt nudged him. "Would you mind playing your trumpet

outside tonight?"

Outside? Brady raised his head. "Why?"

"Ryan texted me last night. His cabin is jealous."

Chris protested. "You get to have your cell phone? That's not fair."

"I have it for emergencies."

"Oh, and that was an emergency?"

Matt ignored him. "He asked if you'd play for his cabin tonight. I figure if you play outside, all the guys' cabins can hear you."

Brady agreed and laid his head down again. Right now, he just wanted to go back to sleep.

"Is everyone finished?" Matt's chair scraped as he stood up. "Okay, men, head back to the cabin and straighten it up." He raised his voice over the moaning. "It doesn't have to be spotless, but if we get the messiest cabin award, I promise to make you regret it. Better hustle. Morning worship starts in 20 minutes. Don't forget your Bibles."

Brady's head popped up. Twenty minutes? *I still have to shower and change.*

***

All morning, one thought kept repeating itself. *What did I do to make Mom send me away?* Throughout morning worship, Brady's mind refused to follow the music. In the small group Bible study that followed, he paid little attention to the lesson about God calling Samuel's name. What terrible thing had he done to make Mom want to get rid of him?

By lunchtime, he still hadn't come up with any ideas. He led Steven through the buffet line then stopped to scan the crowded dining hall for table space.

Claire waved her arm in the air, beckoning him and Steven to her table. She cleared a couple of empty trays. "I

42

grabbed these and set them here to save you some places."

Steven set his tray next to hers and both boys sat down to plates of roast beef and mashed potatoes.

Claire nudged Steven's arm. "I can't believe we're on the same Rec team. First time in all the years we've been coming here."

Steven laughed. "It's about time, but you know I'm not playing ball today. Is Matt around? He was going to find out what Zeke wants me to do instead."

Brady spotted him in the buffet line. "I see him." He stood and waved Matt over to a spot someone else had just left.

Matt put his tray on the table and sat down. "Steven, I've been looking for you. Zeke said Nurse Willie will take you fishing."

"Seriously?" Steven clapped his hands together. "Yesss! Can Brady and Claire come, too?"

"Only if they start having trouble with their eyesight in the next couple of hours. The team needs them. I predict Claire will make a crucial play against the other team and Brady'll hit a game-winning home run. Right?"

Claire pumped her fist. "Yeah."

"Fat chance," Brady muttered. He licked the last of the peach cobbler from his spoon and pushed his tray back. "I've never hit a ball in my life."

Matt pointed his knife at Claire. "I bet she can show you how to do it."

"Nothing to it, Brady." She reached across Steven and tapped Brady's wrist. "Just swing the bat, right?"

"Yeah, right."

Claire looked at him with arched brows. "Okay, that did not sound enthusiastic or confident. We'll work on that first. Are you finished?" She stood and pointed at his tray. "Come on."

"Where are we going?"

"To get some batting practice before the game."

Brady clutched his tray and searched for an excuse. "But what about Steven? I can't just leave him here."

"I'll take him to meet Willie," Matt said.

Brady held up clasped hands to Matt. "Can't I go fishing instead? Pleeease?"

Matt shook his head. "Sorry. You're not in Zeke's orders."

"Are you coming to the game, Matt?" Claire asked.

"Yeah, I'll be there as soon as I deliver Steven."

"Okay, see ya there. Come on, Brady, let's go." Claire took his arm and tugged him out of his chair.

"Later, Brady," Steven called.

"Yeah," Brady muttered as Claire towed him from the dining hall. Given a choice, he'd rather swim in frigid, shark-infested waters than endure this summer version of gym class.

***

Claire called to him from center field. "Dillon's up to bat. Back up. Be ready."

Brady moved deeper into right field, though it was as useless as batting practice. So far, he'd struck out twice. He was unlikely to get on base, but it would be nice to at least hit the ball.

His fielding was just as bad. The one ball that someone hit to right field slipped past his glove and kept rolling. Before he could retrieve it and throw it back to the infield, two runners scored. Now, with Dillon "The Super Jock" up to bat, any hope of Brady stopping the ball was laughable. This guy scored home runs with one leg virtually tied behind his back.

Despite the walking cast on his left leg, Dillon stepped

into the batter's box. His substitute runner stood next to the catcher, poised for take-off. Dillon tapped the bat lightly against his cast.

Brady crossed his fingers. *Don't hit it out here. Please, don't hit it to me.*

The ball left the pitcher's hand, but dropped and bounced before crossing the plate. Dillon lowered his bat while the catcher retrieved the ball and tossed it back to the pitcher.

Brady held his breath as the next pitch flew toward the plate. Dillon let it go by, but when the umpire called it a strike, he wiggled his stance, touched his bat to the corners of home plate and stood ready for the ball. The pitcher released it. Dillon swung.

A split second later, a metallic *tink* sounded across the field. The ball soared over Claire's head to a shallow gully that marked the outfield boundary. Dillon limped along behind his pinch runner for a few steps, then greeted him with a double-handed high-five when the runner crossed home plate. The two exchanged fist bumps with Matt on the sideline. Taylor announced the score.

"Nine. To. One." Heavy emphasis on the nine.

And it's only the third inning. Brady kicked at a dandelion gone to seed, chopping the stem in half. Losing wouldn't be so bad if Taylor didn't rub it in every time his team scored.

The next batter hit a pop fly to the infield, and a swinging strikeout after that brought Brady's team in to bat. He walked to the sideline, calculating his place in the batting order. If everyone ahead of him got out, he could avoid batting this inning.

The first batter cooperated with his plan and struck out. But then it was Claire's turn to bat. It didn't seem right to hope she'd strike out.

"C'mon, Claire. Home run." Two more batters after her meant there was still hope.

Claire swung at the first pitch and missed. The second one came at her and she swung again, connecting this time. She dropped the bat and raced toward first base while the ball rolled past second.

"You made it!" Brady crossed his fingers that the next two batters would strike out. But the pitcher threw four balls, sending the batter to first and Claire to second. After that, a fly ball to right field brought the second out. Claire tagged up and made it safely to third.

Two outs and a possible run on third. Brady's stomach churned as he picked up a bat and dragged it to the batter's box. Dillon knelt behind him, punching a fist into his catcher's glove. With a sigh, Brady raised the bat and let it rest on his shoulder.

"Easy out." Taylor yawned from his position at shortstop. "Hey, Brady, don't bother. You and your team just come on out to the field. Save yourself the embarrassment."

"Shut up, Taylor." Claire kept one toe on third base, her other leg outstretched in a lunge, ready to run.

"He's an idiot. Don't let him get to you." Dillon's voice was barely above a whisper, and Brady wasn't sure whether he'd heard it or imagined it.

He peered back at Dillon, but the catcher simply pounded his glove and nestled his knees into the sandy dirt. Brady shuffled his feet and waited for the first pitch. He swung hard. Missed.

Taylor sat down on the ground and leaned back on his hands. "See, I told you. Easy out."

Brady's face grew hot, a sure sign his ears were turning red.

Dillon whispered as he threw the ball back. "Relax. Take your time."

"Come on, Brady. Hit me home." Claire pumped her fist. "You can do it."

The next pitch came in and he swung the bat around in a lazy arc.

"Aw, c'mon, we're playing softball here, not badminton."

"Taylor, knock it off." Matt called a time out, crooked a finger at Brady, and met him on the sideline. "You don't look like you're having fun."

Brady frowned and narrowed his eyes. "I'd rather be fishing."

"Let me see if I can help." Matt took the bat and swapped it for a lighter one. He demonstrated a proper batting stance and moved Brady's feet and arms into position. "Don't let your bat rest on your shoulder. You want it up slightly, ready to swing."

What I really want is to be done with this.

Matt held his hand out in front of Brady. "Okay, slowly swing the bat straight to my hand."

Brady swung several times, meeting Matt's palm squarely.

"That's good." Matt backed up. "Now, imagine my hand still there but swing hard."

Brady frowned, but swung the bat around.

"Hard," Matt said. "Harder, like you'll break every bone in my body if I make you stay out here any longer."

Brady swung, the force of his anger spinning him around.

"Good! That's what I want to see." Matt patted him on the back. "Now, do the same thing when you see the ball coming. But don't swing unless it comes in about where my hand was."

Brady returned to the batter's box, eyed Matt, and took his

stance. The ball came in low, tempting him to swing and take the out. But the ball fell short of the plate, as did the next pitch.

Throw it, will ya? I want to get out of here. He'd swing at the next pitch no matter what it looked like.

The ball flew toward the plate. Brady set his jaw and swung, putting every ounce of his anger into it. TING! His hands stung and he dropped the bat.

"Yessss!" Matt threw his arms in the air.

Claire screamed. "Run, Brady, run!"

The ball skidded across the infield to Taylor who scooped it up and threw it to first base.

"Out!" The first baseman held it up, then tossed it back to the pitcher.

Still at home plate, Brady turned to Matt, his jaw hanging open.

"I hit it!"

"You sure did." Matt laughed. "Next time, remember to run."

"I really hit it!"

Matt reached out and tousled his hair. "Yeah, you're awesome. But the game's not over yet. Grab a glove now and get out to the field."

Dazed, Brady picked up a glove lying on the ground and jogged toward right field, punching his fist into the glove. "I hit it. I really, really hit it."

Taylor detoured past Brady on his way to the sideline. "You're supposed to run when you hit it. Loser!"

Brady's steps slowed. Who forgets to run when they hit the ball? He gave his glove a half-hearted slap before turning to face the infield. He kicked another dandelion, then ground it into the dirt with his toe.

Claire tapped his shoulder as she ran to center field.

"Great hit, Brady. I knew you could do it."

"Yeah. Sure." He couldn't wait for this stupid game to be over.

CHAPTER 5

Standing out in right field for the better part of an hour almost seemed worth it to enjoy a cool refreshing swim in the lake. Camp didn't seem as bad with the rest of the afternoon spent swimming with Steven, Claire, and Hayley. The moment Steven stepped onto the diving board, Brady sucked in his breath and held it, expecting his friend to go tumbling off the edge. Instead, Steven measured his steps to the end, bounced once, twice, three times and leaped off in a perfect cannonball, making a humongous splash.

Then it was his turn. The diving board wasn't much higher than Brady's top bunk, but it moved and swayed with the motion of the raft. He nearly lost his balance, and looking down made him dizzy. But if Steven could launch himself with such abandon, Brady wasn't about to let fear keep him from jumping. Especially with the girls watching. After that first terrifying plunge, he was hooked.

But free time ended way too soon with the lifeguards sending everyone to their cabins to get ready for supper.

Now Brady's stomach growled as he slid his dinner tray along the buffet line.

Steven laughed. "Hungry?"

"Starved. Feels like I haven't eaten for a week." Brady lifted a spoonful of casserole to his nose and sniffed. "What's this?"

"Monday's supper is always goulash." Steven took a good long whiff. "Yum. And get used to being hungry. Camp does that to you."

Brady sampled a forkful of the casserole on his plate. It tasted better than it looked, and he scooped another spoonful onto his plate. Had he ever felt this hungry before? Must be from all the swimming they'd done after losing the ball game 16-1.

Brady led Steven to an open table, and neither spoke while they filled their stomachs. Brady finished the goulash and carrot sticks and reached for his chocolate cake. His chair juddered backward and he turned to find Taylor using it for support, leaning back on the legs of his own chair.

"Do you mind? I'm trying to eat." Brady pried one of Taylor's fingers off.

"Trying? You must eat about as good as you hit," Taylor sneered.

"I hit the ball. Hit it right to you."

"Yeah, but you forgot to run. How stupid is that?" He yanked Brady's chair again.

"Shut up." Brady glared and jabbed the air near Taylor's fingers with his fork.

Taylor laughed. "Ooh, am I supposed to be scared?"

"Ignore him, Brady," Steven said. "Don't listen to him."

"Yeah, pretend you're deaf. The two of you'd make a great team. He's blind, you're deaf, and you're both dumb." Taylor dropped his chair back onto four legs, cackling and pounding his palms on the table. The boys at his table laughed along with him.

Steven leaned toward Brady. "Seriously, he wants to see you get ticked off. Don't give him the satisfaction."

Brady shoved his dessert plate forward and planted his elbows on the table. "It's not that easy." He clenched his teeth.

"You think I don't know that?" Steven hissed. "You think nobody makes fun of the blind kid?"

"But you just laugh it off."

Steven swallowed his food and laid his fork down. "I do now, but I used to hate it when kids said stuff. It made me so mad I wanted to punch somebody. My dad always told me, 'Sticks and stones may break your bones, but words can never hurt you.' And then I wanted to punch him. One day, Dad told me I have a choice. I can listen when people say stupid things and let them ruin my life, or I can realize they're stupid, ignore it and get on with life."

Brady sucked in a heavy breath. He'd always avoided fights, but right now there was nothing more satisfying than the idea of smashing that nasty grin right to the back of Taylor's head. A tap on his shoulder brought his fist up.

"Whoa! What's that for?" Matt set down his tray and pulled out a chair.

"Sorry," Brady mumbled. "I thought you were someone else."

"Glad I'm not." Matt bowed his head briefly before digging in to his food. "Did you tell Steven you almost hit a home run?"

Steven slapped the table with both hands. "No way! A

home run? You never told me."

Brady rolled his eyes. "Not even close."

"Aw, it wasn't that bad," Matt said. "You hit like that next time, you'll get on base."

"Won't be a next time." Brady reached for his cake again and stuffed half of it into his mouth. He didn't want to talk about it anymore.

Matt turned his attention to Steven. "How was the fishing?"

"I only caught one. Nurse Willie said it was a little blue gill. She didn't catch anything." He tipped his head to one side. "We swam so long this afternoon, I'm waterlogged. I can't get the water out of my ear." He tapped the side of his head with his palm.

"Careful. Your brains might fall out." Taylor picked up his dinner tray and shoved his chair in to squeeze by. His friends followed.

"Taylor, stuff it," Matt warned.

Brady glared at the boys on their way out of the dining hall. Bad enough they teased him; it really irked him when they made Steven the butt of their cruel jokes.

Matt bounced his spoon against Brady's fist. "Is Taylor the reason you were ready to punch me when I sat down? You're not alone. He annoys everybody. Before he pushes your final button, you come tell me about it, y'hear? You vent with me, not him."

Yeah, right. Brady nodded anyway. He gulped the last of his milk and asked Steven if he was ready to go. Matt held up his index finger to stall them.

"Before you guys leave, auditions for Friday night's talent show are right after Rec tomorrow. You think you'd want to try out?"

Brady stiffened. "No thanks."

Steven protested. "What? You'd be the star of the show."

"I'm not here to play a concert. I didn't even bring any music." Brady shook his head.

"So?" Steven shrugged. "I didn't hear any rustling of sheet music when you played 'Amazing Grace' in the cabin yesterday."

Brady frowned, as if Steven could see him.

Matt stuffed a buttered roll in his mouth and mumbled, "Look...you don't have to do this...but you really are talented on that trumpet." He swallowed. "Steven's right. You'd rock this place. Think about it, okay?"

Brady rolled his eyes and exhaled loudly. "Okay."

"Great!" Steven said. "You have until the end of Rec tomorrow to think about it. And think yes. Got it? Yes. Yes."

This was a mistake. No doubt about it.

***

Brady, Steven, and Claire claimed their seats early for the evening worship session. Kids swarmed the front rows like gnats around a porch light, squeezing shoulder to shoulder into the wooden pews. Even the air clung close. No breeze sifted through the screened windows or drifted down from the ceiling fans turning in sluggish circles. Sweat trickled down Brady's back as he sang and clapped along with the band's music. A certain odor wafting among the close-packed bodies suggested someone needed deodorant.

He'd been so busy today that the memory of what happened with Mom had retreated to the shadowy corners of his mind. Was it really only yesterday? It seemed longer, until her angry words slashed through him again. *I don't want you...* She'd threatened to send him to his dad once or twice in recent months. Both times, he'd thought it odd, knowing how she felt

55

about his dad. He never believed she was serious, but now he was curious. *Had she planned this all along? Is that why I had to go to camp?*

He backed away from that thought and returned his attention to the front where the band had finished. Everyone sat down, and the room grew quiet when Zeke hopped onto the stage.

"Last night, we learned the difference between knowing about God and knowing him personally." The director moved the easel to center stage and drew a red heart that filled the page. In the upper left lobe, he wrote 'God.'

"Raise your hand if you believe God loves us."

Steven, Claire, and most of the other campers raised their hands high. Brady raised his no higher than his head.

"We may believe God loves *us*," he spread his arms out as if to hug everyone at once, "but we don't know it as a personal love. For example, do you believe he loves you, Michelle?" Zeke pointed to a girl on the front row. She nodded, and he added + *Michelle* under God's name inside the heart.

"Casey, do you believe your name is in there?" The boy answered yes and Zeke wrote + *Casey* under Michelle's name.

Brady wiggled in the seat, unable to get comfortable. He couldn't picture his name inside that heart. His dad didn't love him enough to stick around, and now his mom didn't want him either. Why would God love him?

Zeke added several more names to the heart, and then asked, "Hannah, how do you know God loves you?"

"Because..." The girl's gaze roamed about the walls and ceiling, as if the answer were written there. "Because the Bible says so." It sounded more like a question than a statement.

"That's one way. How do you know someone loves you? Let's say, your parents. How do you know they love you?"

Zeke repeated answers from other campers. "They buy you clothes, video games, cell phones. They provide a home, make sure you have a place to live."

Brady's stomach twisted. He slouched down into the seat, wishing he could disappear.

"They feed you too." Zeke called on one of the counselors. "Nate, did your mother ever forget to feed you?"

Nate patted his hefty stomach and shook his head from side to side, a satisfied grin across his face.

Zeke opened his Bible. "In Isaiah chapter 49, God asks if a mother could forget to feed her baby or have no compassion on her child.'"

Brady crossed his arms; if he didn't hold himself together, he might fall apart.

Zeke continued reading. "Though she may forget, I will not forget you! See,' he says, 'I have engraved you on the palms of my hands.'" Zeke closed the Bible and laid it on the stage. "When I was dating my wife, I used to write her name on my hand with a pen. Anybody still do that?"

Whistles and laughter rose from the back. Steven turned toward the sound. "What's going on?"

Brady pushed himself up to look for the cause of the disturbance. "Some kid wrote a girl's name on his hand. They're holding his hand in the air for Zeke to see." He scrunched back down in his seat.

Zeke grinned and held up his own hand. "I wrote my wife's name on my hand to make it feel like she was always close by. Whenever we were apart, I'd look at her name, curl my fingers around it, and pretend I was holding her hand. But I had a problem. Every time I washed my hands, her name disappeared."

Zeke pointed to his drawing. "Your name isn't written in

chalk that washes away. It's engraved permanently on God's hands." He moved his finger about his palm like an engraving needle. Then he tore off the sheet of paper with the heart, letting it fall to the side, and began scribbling dark outlines on a fresh sheet of paper.

The room buzzed with hushed voices as campers tried to guess what he was drawing. Brady described the emerging picture to Steven: facial features, a colorful sports jersey, and finally, a basketball in the figure's hand.

"Who recognizes this superstar?" Zeke asked. Several boys shouted a name.

"Who's that?" Steven asked.

Brady shrugged. "Don't ask me."

Claire rolled her eyes. "Seriously? You guys don't know the star of the Miami Heat?" She shook her head.

"What do you see on his arms when he plays?" Zeke asked.

Claire joined the chorus of voices. "Tattoos!"

Using a black permanent marker, Zeke scribbled up and down the figure's arms. Then he rubbed his hands together and faced the campers.

"Even tattoos fade when they get old. God didn't use chalk or a permanent marker. He didn't tattoo your name on his hands. He engraved your name."

He pointed to individual campers. "Your name, and yours, and yours is engraved on the palm of his hand. Now that's what I call a personal love."

***

The light outside the cabin door cast a yellow glow around the steps. Brady stumbled over a tree root as he moved beyond the circle's glow. What was it about this bedtime ritual that appealed to Matt and the other counselors? At least it gave him a chance to get out of the cabin alone, if only for a few minutes. He found a spot beneath the nearest oak tree and faced the cabins with his trumpet in hand. Open windows allowed every inside noise to carry through the night air, whether voices or body functions.

Brady put the trumpet to his lips and played the familiar song. The noise from the cabins dimmed and the lights flickered out. The last notes lingered until they evaporated into the stillness. Even the crickets remained silent afterward.

Brady drank in the solitude. Sharing quarters with eleven other boys made him thankful he was an only child. Camp activities left him no time to play his trumpet, except for now. He missed experimenting with notes and rhythms and sounds. It calmed him, helped him think, brought his jumbled thoughts into order the way arranging notes on a staff made a melody. He held the trumpet close to his chest.

If only he didn't have to go back into the cabin. Brady toyed with the idea of walking away. Just head for home and never come back. Except he didn't have a home anymore. He threw his head back and whispered to the heavens, "Doesn't anyone care?"

A single star blinked back at him. Only one? But he was standing under the tree's canopy. A small gap among the branches must have allowed this one star to peek through. One lonely star. *Just like me.*

"Brady?" Matt called from the cabin's doorway. "You planning to spend the night out there?"

"I'm coming," he answered, with little enthusiasm.

Brady dragged the squeaky screen door open. The only light burning in the cabin spilled from Matt's room. Brady laid his trumpet in its case and made his way along the aisle to his bunk. Thankfully, Taylor remained quiet while Matt stood in the bunkroom's doorway.

"Good night, men. Remember, there will be ugly consequences for anyone making noise after lights out." Matt went into his room, but left his door slightly ajar.

Brady climbed to his top bunk, ignoring the whispers and snickering that began almost immediately. He lay on his back and stared into the darkness, thinking about Zeke's story of writing his wife's name on his hand to make her seem closer. Would it work? Taking care to move in silence, he climbed down to the floor again and dug through his stuff until his fingers closed around a pen.

Steven whispered to him. "What are you doing?"

"Nothing. Just forgot something." He scrambled back up to sit on his bunk. Straining to see in the scant light from Matt's room, he wrote the letters M-o-m on his left palm. He shoved the pen under his pillow and lay back, curling his fingers over what he'd written.

His eyes closed, but the rest of Zeke's message swirled through his brain. *Does God really love me? Enough to engrave my name on his hands?* He reached for the pen again and leaned on his right elbow, taking the pen in his left hand. With some difficulty, he drew three awkward letters on his right palm. G-o-d.

Drowsiness settled over him and he nestled his head back onto the pillow. His eyes closed and he fell asleep, one hand holding the other over his heart.

CHAPTER 6

Brady lifted one eyelid halfway when Steven's rustlings awakened him. Dust particles drifted and sparkled in a shaft of morning light. Yawning, he stretched one arm up and spread his fingers wide. A glimpse of his palm snapped him awake. He shoved his hand under his pillow and jerked his head around to make sure no one else had seen it. But the other boys were still asleep and Steven couldn't see anything.

Brady dropped his head back onto his pillow. Plenty of time to get to the bathroom and wash the lettering off before anyone noticed. He moved both hands into his sleeping bag to hide them, but held the bag open, using his right index finger to trace the letters on his left hand. *Does Mom miss me at all?* She'd still be asleep at this hour. She used to get up early to enjoy a quiet cup of coffee and watch the sun come up. He missed her morning smile and the quiet talks they'd have while he ate breakfast. He frowned, trying to remember when she started sleeping late. Sometime after Christmas, after she had married Richard. By the end of the school year, Brady had almost gotten used to eating breakfast alone and letting himself out the door.

He closed his eyes, wishing he could go back to sleep, back to being unaware of the emptiness in the pit of his stomach. He hated waking up, especially those first moments when the fact that he didn't have a home anymore slammed into his brain.

"Your dad will pick you up on Saturday." Seriously? Dad doesn't even drive across town to see me.

Steven mumbled to himself as he got dressed, and Brady tried to imagine what it was like having a dad around to watch out for you or teach you to paddle a canoe. No memories came to mind of his own Dad ever spending time with him.

"You awake?" Steven's hand sought Brady's shoulder. "Let's go. I'm starved."

His eyes flew open. Steven stood by his bunk, showered and dressed, hair combed, dark glasses in place. Not only that, but he'd made enough noise getting dressed to wake up everyone else. Brady kicked off his sleeping bag and hustled into the shower. Minutes later, he'd thrown on shorts and a wrinkled t-shirt, finger-combed his hair so it wasn't sticking up, and checked his hands one more time.

Steven waited at the door, his fingers tapping an impatient rhythm on the wood frame. Brady led him outside and down the steps where he caught a whiff of bacon. Its mouthwatering aroma hung in the muggy air, the way it did at the pancake restaurant near his house.

"I think my stomach just woke up. Let's move it." Brady quickened their pace. Soon their trays held plates loaded with scrambled eggs, toast, jelly and bacon.

Janie brought out a fresh pan of eggs and greeted them across the buffet. "That's what I like to see, boys with an appetite." She squinted at Brady. "You look half asleep. Is Steven keeping you up at night?"

Brady grinned at her. "No, but he does get me up way too early."

"Hey, isn't Janie's cooking worth it?"

She winked at Brady. "He's buttering me up for something."

Steven laughed. "Extra brownies tonight? Please?"

Janie pointed a large metal serving spoon at Steven, but looked at Brady. "What did I tell you?"

Brady laughed, picked up his tray and led Steven toward the tables. Claire waved them over to where she sat with Hayley. She didn't even wait for them to sit down before blurting out her news.

"I found out we're doing the water carnival for Rec today."

Steven's head jerked up. "Today? But it's only Tuesday."

"Our counselor told us another group is renting some of the canoes tomorrow for a river trip the rest of the week. So they switched the carnival to today. You guys want to do the canoe race with me?"

"Sure." Steven bit into a piece of bacon.

Brady spread some jelly on his toast. "Three of us?"

"Yeah, we'll represent the whole Rec team."

Steven nodded. "It's fun. We've both done it before so you'll be with pros. No worries."

***

The water carnival kicked off after lunch with a tug-o-war competition in the shallow part of the swimming area. Jason, the head lifeguard, supervised from the pier. His teeth clenched a whistle poised to signal a team's victory. He paced the pier, staying even with the bandana tied to the rope's middle. It inched close to one goal then shifted the other way.

Steven and Claire held the first two positions on the red team's side of the rope. They bellowed instructions and encouragement to the rest of the team.

"Pull! Harder! Keep it strong."

Farther back, Brady pulled behind Chris in waist- high water. The wet rope skidded through his hands. He dug his heels into the sandy bottom, but lost his footing. His feet slipped forward, taking out Chris as well and dunking them both underwater.

He stood and wiped the water from his face. "This is impossible."

Chris righted himself, and wound his arm over and under the rope for a better grip. "Just keep pulling."

Brady grimaced, braced himself again, and followed Chris's example for gripping the rope. They'd lost a little ground, but soon recovered, only to lose it again. Moments later, Jason's whistle blasted.

Amid the other team's wild cheers, Claire consoled them. "Hey, second place is not bad."

If they had to lose, he'd much rather do it this way than by chasing a ball around a field. His arms and legs were tired, but it was a good tired as he slogged through the water with Steven, Claire and Chris. Other teams were already lining up on the beach for the wet sweatshirt relay, and they threaded their way through the tangle of campers. As they looked for their assembly spot, a familiar voice called out, "Hey, the losers are back."

Claire stopped in front of Taylor and planted her hands on her hips. "Not this time. We lasted longer in the tug-o-war than you. Know what that makes you? Loo-ser." She formed an L with her thumb and forefinger and held it against her forehead.

Brady couldn't help grinning at her singsong taunt. If only he had Claire's confidence and boldness.

They found their team's spot on the beach, and Brady took a position behind Claire as they lined up on the sand. Unable to participate in this event, Steven stood to the side, giving the team a pep talk. Ahead of Claire, Chris stood first in line, his toes nudging the rope that marked the starting point. A counselor handed out a sweatshirt to each team.

"Is everybody ready?" Jason paced the pier, waiting for a response, his voice ragged through the bullhorn. "I said, are you ready?"

This time, whoops and cheers answered him.

"Each team should have a sweatshirt. If you're the first one in line, put it on now."

Chris held up the navy sweatshirt. "It's 200 degrees out here. And this thing is huge."

"Just put it on," Claire ordered.

Brady didn't envy Chris. Even when a cloud blocked the sun, the air pressed in heavy and sticky. Across the lake, clouds gathered as if preparing for their own relay.

Chris's knees peeked out from beneath the hem band of the sweatshirt. He spread his arms and twirled the sleeve ends that fell several inches beyond the tips of his fingers.

"All right. Listen up!" Jason barked instructions. "When I give the signal, the first person in line will make their way out here, slap the pier and return. Failure to touch the pier will disqualify you."

"He's not joking," Claire warned. "Slap it hard so he hears it."

Jason continued. "When you return, your feet must cross

the rope before you transfer the sweatshirt to the next person on your team. Make sure your head is through the neck, and both arms are through the sleeves before you start into the water or you'll be called back. When everyone on your team has finished, sit down.

You will not be counted until your whole team is sitting. All right? On your mark. Get set."

He paused and two teams jumped to a false start. When they returned to position, he yelled, "Go!"

Chris raced into the water, holding the hem up and high-stepping through the shallows. When his knees no longer cleared the surface, he plunged in. The water roiled with six contestants beating their way through to slap the pier and return. Shouts filled the air as teams urged their respective players to Swim! Run! Hurry!

"Go, Chris!" Claire screamed, jumping up and down.

Brady cheered as Chris slapped the pier then pushed himself backward into the water for his return.

"How's he doing?" Steven shouted.

Brady barely heard him over the noise and commotion. "He's ahead."

Moments later, Chris rose from the shallow water and hurried for the beach. As soon as his feet touched the rope, he pulled the waterlogged garment over his head and dropped it onto the sand.

"Don't just drop it." Claire grabbed the sweatshirt and shook it, spattering her teammates with wet sand. She struggled to pull it over her head and shove her arms through the inside-out wet sleeves. "There's a trick to this. I'll show you when I get back." Spitting sand, she raced into the churning water.

"Is she ahead?" Steven sounded as breathless as if he were

participating.

"Yeah, but not by much." Brady called out encouragement as Claire slapped the pier, turned and swam hard toward shore. "Here she comes."

Claire reached out to him as she crossed the rope. "Brady, grab my hands. Bend over like this." She bent at the waist, pulling Brady toward her until their heads knocked together.

"Ouch!" The softness of her hands in his erased the pain in his head.

The rest of the team followed Claire's instructions, grabbing the hem of the sweatshirt and peeling it from her body directly onto Brady. The wet garment clung to him like some sort of thick plastic wrap. Claire pushed him forward and he stumbled into the water, waiting until it reached his thighs before diving under.

His arms strained against the waterlogged sleeves, reminding him of bad dreams where something scary is chasing him, but his feet only move in slow motion. He came up for air and got a mouthful of turbulent water. Choking and spitting, Brady pushed ahead the last few yards. He pounded his fist on the pier and turned back toward shore, alternately plunging into the water, standing up to take a few steps, then plunging in again.

Claire and Chris waited for him just across the rope. They transferred the sweatshirt to the next teammate and sent her off. Brady picked up his towel, wiped his face and the grit from his mouth and tried to catch his breath. He spit a couple times to get rid of the lake taste.

"How are we doing?" Steven asked.

Brady studied the other teams. "We're still ahead, but now others are using Claire's trick too. It'll be close." His stomach began to clench with dread that Taylor's team might catch up.

Soon, the last of their team members crossed the rope. Brady, Claire and the rest dropped to the sand and raised their arms in victory. Claire pulled Steven to the ground. "You're part of the team. Sit."

Jason blew his whistle, pointed at them and held up his index finger. Immediately his whistle sounded again and he pointed two fingers at another team.

"We did it!" Claire cheered. "We won! Where's Taylor?" She stood and called his name, holding up one finger and doing a little victory dance in the sand.

Taylor scowled and turned away.

Brady laughed. If only he could make Taylor glower the way Claire did.

CHAPTER 7

When all the teams finished the race, the three friends gathered up their towels and joined the crowd exiting the beach. As the next event was announced, they moved up to the grassy hill where Dillon watched the competition by himself. Claire threw her towel on the ground and dropped down beside him. Brady shook the sand from his soggy towel before he and Steven sat on it.

Dillon shifted his leg with the cast on it and congratulated them. "Nice win."

Claire hugged her knees. "Thanks. Is this torture for you, watching all this and not being part of it?"

"Just about." Dillon gave her a half-smile. "Now I know how you must feel, Steven."

Steven shrugged. "Yeah, but I get to do some of the events. I heard about your cast. What happened?"

"Broke my ankle in a soccer game. I'm supposed to get it

off next week, but I didn't want to miss camp."

"Aw, so close. Too bad you couldn't get it off earlier." Steven lifted his face to the breeze. "Rain's coming."

Brady squinted up at the sun. "How can you tell?"

"The air is changing." Steven sniffed. "Smells like rain. Hope it holds off 'til we're finished."

Claire shielded her eyes with her hand. "I think you're right. It looks kinda dark across the lake."

"What's going on down there?" Brady drew their attention to Ryan who was wading from the boat dock to the swimming pier. He approached Jason, pointing at the clouds across the lake.

Steven cocked his head to the side. "Tell me what's happening."

Claire explained. "Looks like those clouds have Ryan and Jason worried."

Moments later, Ryan returned to his boats, and Jason spoke into the bullhorn.

"All right, we need to speed things up a little. Any teams not currently participating in the relay here need to head to the boat dock. The canoe race will start in five minutes."

"That's us." Claire hopped up and grabbed her towel. "Let's go, guys."

Dillon wished them luck, and the three started for the boat dock. Claire ran ahead to claim a canoe.

Brady took three lifejackets from Ryan and handed one to Steven. "What about paddles?"

"No paddles." Steven buckled the strap on his lifejacket and adjusted the length.

Brady frowned. "How are we supposed to…"

Steven held his hands in the air and wiggled his fingers.

Claire called. "Steven, come get in front." She'd already

maneuvered a canoe into knee-deep water and was holding on to keep it from drifting. As they approached, she asked Brady, "You want middle or back?"

"Middle." Surely Claire knew how to steer, even without paddles. He handed her a life jacket and pulled his own orange vest over his head. As soon as Steven settled into the bow, Brady climbed into position.

"There's a trick to this, too." Claire spoke into his ear, startling him. But he kind of liked being so close to her.

"Steven already knows this, but you don't," she said. "Everyone gets jammed up trying to get around the buoy. We'll go farther out where there'll be room to turn. Then once we turn, we'll shoot straight back here. Got it?"

Brady nodded. The starting line-up had five other teams. Did they strategize their race, too? At the far end, Taylor climbed into the bow of his canoe. Their eyes met and a slow grin spread across Taylor's face. He turned and said something to his teammates, and they all aimed sly grins his way.

They're planning something. But his team had a plan too. He liked Claire's idea, liked the way she took on challenges, facing them head-on rather than letting things happen to her. If only he could be more like her. *Maybe I can.* He waited for Taylor to look his way and returned the smirk.

Ryan's whistle brought everyone to attention. "Listen up! I think we can finish this before that storm closes in, but just in case, I want every canoe to carry paddles. If you see lightning or hear any thunder or a long blast on my whistle, forget the race, grab those paddles and hustle back here. Understand?"

He distributed paddles to each team, explaining the rules as he went along. Sit or kneel only. No standing. Life jackets always on and secured. No holding onto or ramming another canoe. First team out around the buoy and back wins.

"Ready? Set?"

The whistle blasted and Claire shoved the canoe forward. It bobbed a little when she hopped in. Brady got up on his knees, his hands reaching into the water, pulling back hard and fast, first on one side then the other. The momentum from Claire's push only carried them quickly for several yards before they slowed almost to a stop.

"We're not getting anywhere," Brady yelled. One or two of the other canoes appeared to be moving. Another had turned sideways, and the team was working hard to point it back toward the buoy.

Steven called over his shoulder. "Pull together. Claire, call the strokes."

Claire took charge. "Brady, on your right. Steven, stay left. Stroke. Stroke. Stroke."

At last, the canoe began to move forward. The lake breeze had already picked up strength, mustering waves that slapped the canoe and splattered drops on his face. The aluminum hull was wet from his feet when he climbed in, and it gave him no traction. His knees slipped and slid forward, back, sideways. He lifted one knee and– Ouch! –landed on the buckle from the strap of his life vest. No time now to secure the straps. He tossed the buckle out of his way, grabbed his towel from the crossbar thwart and threw it down to kneel on. He still slid a bit, but at least it was a soft slide.

All six canoes meandered like turtles toward the buoy. Two teams nosed ahead, but with the slow pace it would be a tight race. Brady's team would have to power it up to win. He dug his right hand deep into the water, wincing as the edge of the canoe bit into the soft underside of his upper arm.

Teams shouted instructions to each other, their voices competing with those from the event in the swimming area.

Claire dropped back to calling every other stroke and finally called only an occasional correction when they lost their common rhythm. Two lead canoes reached the buoy and began turning just as a third team approached from the buoy's opposite side. There was the beginning of the traffic jam Claire talked about.

"Keep going. Don't let up yet." Claire urged them past the congestion then directed their turn.

"Steven, keep pulling forward. Brady, paddle backward."

Ever so slowly, the canoe swung in a wide arc and straightened out for the return trip.

"Okay, forward all. Move it." Claire resumed calling the strokes.

Brady's arm and shoulder ached, but he couldn't slow down now. They needed to get past the buoy before any of the other teams broke free of the jam. Closer to shore, Taylor was lying atop the bow deck of his canoe. They hadn't even reached the buoy yet. *So much for their plans of sabotage.* Brady smiled to himself.

The buoy drew nearer, coming up on his left. Just a few more yards and they'd be in the clear, heading for the dock and another victory.

Just then, a canoe broke free of the jam and moved straight into their path. "Noo-o-o!" he cried. "Hard left!" Why couldn't they use the paddles instead of this useless hand rowing that took forever to get anywhere?

"Switch sides," Claire yelled. "Steven, push out. Brady, fast forward."

He leaned over the left side and dug both hands into the water, tipping the canoe and nearly pitching himself into the lake.

Steven cried out and grabbed hold of the sides. "Whoa!

Hang on."

"Watch it," Claire scolded.

"I'm sorry!" Chastised, Brady settled lower, bracing one hand on the thwart in front of him while scooping water back with the other. The canoe inched to the left at a snail's speed. As they closed in on the other canoe, Brady leaned away from it as if that would help. With little more than a foot to spare, they slipped past and Claire pressed them forward again.

"Let's go! Stroke. Stroke."

They passed the buoy and Brady chuckled at the sight of Taylor's canoe sitting parallel to shore. They'd never make it to the buoy if they couldn't even head in the right direction.

Another canoe threatened to pull even with them. He took a deep breath and dug in for the sprint home. A drop of water hit his cheek, another on his back, his shoulder. *Rain.* The sky had grown overcast since they set out. The wind had picked up too, blowing against their backs now, helping them along.

Forget the weather. *Focus.* Brady fixed his attention on the shore, his mind on whatever it took to get there. Reach forward and down, pull back, lift. Repeat. Faster. From the corner of his eye, a movement distracted him again. Just a quick look. Taylor's canoe bore down on them.

"They're using paddles!"

A wicked smile played across Taylor's face, and the high-pitched whoops and cheers of his teammates carried above the shouts of the other teams. In perfect cadence, they plunged their paddles into the water and raked them back.

Brady's gut told him this would hurt. "They're ramming us. Watch out!"

"Hang on," Claire cried.

The impact knocked Brady to the side. Metal grated against metal. Before he could recover, the canoe rocked, throwing him to the other side. Taylor's hands gripped the edge of the canoe and he leaned on the gunwale, tipping it down toward the water. He let up then pushed down again, rocking the canoe from side to side.

"Cut it out!" Brady struggled to regain his balance.

Claire screamed. "You're such a loser, Taylor. Stop it!"

Steven clenched the sides of the canoe and yelled over his shoulder, "What are you doing?"

Taylor laughed. "Just making sure you don't win." He shoved hard on the gunwale again. It dipped dangerously close to the water's surface.

Brady struggled for traction on the hull while Claire landed a fist on Taylor's fingers then tried to pry them off. Steven braced himself against both gunwales and tried to climb back over his seat. But the next pitch of the canoe threw him into Brady.

Brady grunted and squirmed out from under Steven. "I'll get him. You try to balance us."

Taylor's grasp on the gunwale held firm despite Claire's efforts. Brady added his fist, pounding Taylor's fingers repeatedly. He tried to pull him into a headlock, or grab hold of his shoulder, but his wet hands slipped from his tormentor's shirtless body. Finally, he caught Taylor's upper arm and yanked, pulled, anything to drag Taylor off the bow deck. The canoe rocked more violently. Taylor's hand gripped his neck, pulling him forward, pushing down. The canoe tilted. Brady reached for something to keep from falling and gripped nothing but air.

"Aaaah!" Water swallowed him, cutting short his cry. It gushed into his nose and mouth. He coughed, only to inhale more water as he tried to suck in air. Brady kicked and thrashed, unable to tell which direction was up, his life jacket useless. Where was his life jacket? It must have come off. He'd never fastened the strap.

Brady needed air now. His arms were like Jell-O after all the paddling. Still, he pushed through the water, diving deeper into an underwater jungle. Wrong way. The water looked lighter in the other direction.

The urge to cough, to breathe, was overwhelming. *Am I going to drown? Would Mom even miss me?* He fought against panic until his head hit something hard and he gasped, forcing more precious air from his lungs. Canoe! He shoved sideways and seconds later his head breached the surface.

Brady coughed, gagged, gulped air and coughed some more. A long whistle blast followed by several short ones echoed across the lake. With all the water in his ears, he couldn't tell what all the shouting was about. But the annoying laughter from somewhere close by was clear enough. His canoe—minus his teammates—sat upright, though very low in the water.

"Claire? Steven!" His voice was frantic.

"Right here." Steven spit out lake water. His dark glasses clung stubbornly to one ear.

"Are you..." Cough. "...okay?"

"Peachy." Steven's tone was flat. "You?"

"Lost my lifejacket. What about Claire?"

Just then, her voice screeched from the other side of Taylor's canoe.

"Taayyloor! Aauerggh! You are so. . . so. . . ."

"Enjoy your swim," Taylor taunted. He and his friends back-paddled, then turned toward shore.

"Everyone all right out there?" Ryan's voice squawked through a bullhorn. "Steven? Claire? Brady?" He waited to hear from each of them then called out instructions. "Your

76

canoe won't sink, so hang on to it until I get there in the motorboat. The rest of you grab your paddles and get in here now. Pull your canoe up, put away your equipment and head to your cabins. Except Taylor's team. I expect you three to be sitting right here on this dock when I get back."

"Where exactly is the canoe?" Steven asked.

"You're facing it. Swim forward, just a couple strokes." Brady spotted his life jacket floating near the canoe and swam to it. He ducked his head into it then floated on his back to pull the strap around his body and snap the buckle.

"I'm going to kill him," Claire vowed as she swam up to take hold of the canoe.

A wave washed over Brady, setting off another bout of coughing and gagging.

"Are you okay?" Steven asked.

Brady coughed and nodded. "I'll live. I think." He turned his back to the wind and waves and clung to the side of the canoe. Another cough convulsed him.

"You sure you're all right?" Claire moved around the canoe, closer to him.

He took a deep breath and stifled another urge to cough. "Yeah, I'm okay."

Moments later, Ryan circled and cut the engine as he pulled up in the motorboat. He threw a towrope to Brady.

"Tie this to the front of the canoe. Make it tight."

Brady grabbed the rope and moved around Steven. His fingers pressed the nylon rope through the eye and tied a knot.

Claire helped Steven find the motorboat ladder and they both climbed aboard. Her protests started even before her feet touched the top of the ladder. "Are we disqualified? We better not be. This was not our fault."

"I know. Not much I can do about it now." Ryan tugged

on the rope to check Brady's knot. "Tighter. Make a couple more knots."

Claire persisted. "Can't we try again in the second round?"

"Not gonna be a second round."

"Why not?"

Ryan looked up as a rumble sounded overhead. "That's why. Okay, Brady, get yourself up here. Let's go."

Startled by the thunder, Brady hurried to the ladder. Angry dark clouds were nearly on top of them as he joined the others.

Dripping and shivering in the wind, Claire positioned herself beside Ryan who knelt on the driver's seat. "Did you see him tip us over?"

"I did. We'll be having a not-so-friendly chat as soon as I get everything secured. I'm sure Zeke will want some words with them too. But right now, you need to sit so we can get out of here." He eased the throttle forward and headed for the dock, keeping one eye on the canoe behind them.

Lightning brightened the clouds as Brady stepped off the boat. Moments later, thunder rolled. They'd be lucky to get back to the cabin before it all broke loose. The other canoes had been pulled up on shore and tipped over so they wouldn't fill with rain. Taylor and his two friends sat by themselves on the dock, dangling their feet in the water. Brady glared at them.

The two teammates snickered and whispered between themselves. Taylor appeared to study the water dripping from his toes while whistling a soft, tuneless melody. The whistling stopped as Brady, Steven and Claire walked past.

"Loo-sers," Taylor sing-songed under his breath.

Claire planted her foot on Taylor's back and shoved him

off the dock into waist-high water. "You're the biggest loser around here."

Taylor's buddies guffawed and pointed. "You gonna let a girl do that to you?"

Taylor spun around, dousing everyone as he splashed and threw water with his cupped hands.

"Oh, like that's going to do anything," Claire retorted.

"We're already wet, stupid. You're such an idiot." Brady wiped his face with his sopping wet towel.

Steven nudged him on ahead. "Come on, guys. Let's go."

Ryan interrupted the exchange by summoning Taylor and his buddies to empty out the canoe and pull it up on the shore.

Brady hung his and Steven's wet life jackets alongside Claire's in the boathouse. She continued complaining as the three of them climbed the steps.

"Taylor deserves to be sent home for that." She slung her towel around her shoulders.

"Zeke won't send him home," Steven said. "He'll just make him memorize a Bible verse and probably restrict him from the fun stuff for a day or two."

"Is that all?" Brady jumped at a blinding flash of lightning, followed by a vibrating roll of thunder. Fat drops of rain beat against his body. "We need to go. You ready, Steven?"

"Yep. Later, Claire."

She was already scurrying toward her cabin.

CHAPTER 8

Brady sprawled on his bunk, trying to think of something to do. The thunder and lightning had passed, but rain still beat a steady rhythm on the roof. He stretched his aching arms. Some bluish bruising already showed where they'd scraped against the canoe. But he liked the way his tired muscles burned. Wouldn't it be cool if he looked buff by the time camp ended? He turned his back to the rest of the bunks and flexed his biceps. They looked bigger to him. Would anyone else notice?

The screen door creaked then slammed shut. Matt's voice called to him.

"Brady? Steven? Are you here?"

"Yeah." They both answered at once, and Brady rolled over to see what Matt wanted.

The counselor hurried in and stood beside their bunks, wet hair and t-shirt plastered to his body. A puddle formed at his feet. "I heard what happened. You guys okay?"

Steven answered first. "I'm good."

"Yeah, we're fine." Brady nodded. "Where's Taylor?"

"He's with Zeke right now. I'm just making sure you guys are all right. You don't need to see Nurse Willie or anything?"

Brady shook his head.

"Okay. Well then, I guess I'll go find some dry clothes." Matt gave his head a vigorous shake, sprinkling the boys with water.

"Hey!" Brady jerked back from the shower.

Ignoring their protests, Matt laughed all the way to his room.

Brady rubbed the moisture from his arms and lay back on his pillow. Two bunks over, Chris and Nick debated mid-season major league baseball standings. Across the room, a raucous card game was in session. It would be the perfect time to practice his trumpet, but he didn't want to disturb the other guys. Besides, he'd rather play where others couldn't hear him, in case he messed up.

Steven stood up next to the bunk. "I bought a postcard for my mom. If I tell you what to say, will you write it for me?"

"Sure." Brady swung down and settled onto the foot of Steven's bed. He took the postcard and used his teeth to pull the cap off a pen. Leaning back against the bunk frame, he crossed his legs. "Okay, I'm ready."

Steven sat at the other end of the bed and dictated. "Hi, Mom. Having lots of fun this week." He punched his pillow up and wiggled into a comfortable position before continuing. "The water carnival was today. We won the sweatshirt relay and almost won the canoe race, but another team rammed us and tipped us over. Reminded me of Dad. Love, Steven." He paused until Brady finished writing. "Does that sound okay?"

"You think she'll worry about you getting tipped over?"

"Yeah, you're right. Better cross out the part about getting tipped over. How much room do I have left?"

Brady scribbled over the offending sentence to make it unreadable. "Maybe one more sentence."

"P.S. Brady is writing this for me. See you on Saturday." Steven sat up straight. "Sorry, that's two. Does it fit?"

"Jus-s-st barely." Brady put in the final period and held it up for inspection. "What's your address?"

Steven recited his address. "Now, you want me to write one for you? Oh, wait. Your mom probably can't read Braille."

"Ha-ha." Brady didn't care to find the humor in Steven's joke. As he climbed back up to his bed, Steven made another offer.

"I do have an extra postcard if you want it."

"No, thanks." He laid his head on his pillow and stared up at the roof beams, wondering what his mom was doing, or thinking, at that moment.

Steven popped up beside his bunk, postcard in hand. "How about sending it to your dad?"

"I don't want your stupid postcard!" He tore it from Steven's hand and tossed it to the floor.

"I just thought, since your dad's picking you up..."

"Don't believe it. It's not gonna happen."

Steven's brows puckered. "What do you mean?"

Brady expelled his breath and spoke through clenched teeth. "He doesn't care about me. He's never wanted me around. All he cares about is his work."

Steven's head sank against the bed frame. "I thought having my dad die was bad. That stinks." He raised his head again. "What are you going to do? You have to live somewhere."

"I don't know. I'll think of something." Brady swallowed

hard, hating the idea that a blind kid whose dad died felt sorry for him. He sat up and changed the subject. "Since you know this place so well, where's a good place to practice my horn?"

Steven jerked upright. "Wait, what time is it?"

"Not even close to suppertime."

"Who cares about supper? I'm talking tryouts. You need to get over to the chapel."

Brady's shoulders dropped. "Steven, I don't want…"

"Too bad. You can't sit around feeling sorry for yourself." Steven stuck his head around the end of the bunk. "Hey, Matt. Brady needs his trumpet."

"But it's raining," Brady protested.

"So? You've been wet before. You just said you wanted to practice." Steven moved out to the aisle. "Hey! How many of you guys think Brady should try out for the talent show?"

Cheers and whistles filled the cabin. Matt whistled too as he carried Brady's trumpet into the bunkroom.

"You hear that? Your fans demand it." Steven stood at attention, his right hand raised in a salute. "We poor fools, so lacking in talent, are counting on you to uphold the pride of Oaks Cabin. It's a big job, but we're confident you can do it. Go forth and conquer!"

Amid more whistles and applause, Brady couldn't help smiling at his friend's silly act. Maybe Steven was right. Anything was better than sitting here feeling sorry for himself. He climbed down from the bunk and took the trumpet case from Matt.

"Wait a minute." Steven felt for his suitcase, opened it, and rummaged along the side. "You want this?" He held out a compact umbrella that was red with white polka dots.

Brady looked at Matt and rolled his eyes. "No. And if I were you, I'd lose that thing as soon as possible."

Steven shrugged. "I didn't want it anyway. Mom put it in." He tossed the umbrella back and snapped the suitcase shut. "Okay, break a leg."

"I think that's for actors."

"So? Act like you're leaving. Knock 'em dead."

Brady stopped at the screen door and peered outside. Heavy clouds made it look more like evening than mid-afternoon. The neighboring cabin was almost invisible in the downpour. Tree branches sagged with the weight of rain on their leaves. Everything smelled wet. He pushed the door open and rain pelted the concrete steps, splashing onto his ankles and legs. He ducked his head, hugged the trumpet case to his chest, and bolted for the chapel.

Seconds later, he reached the door, but his clothes were drenched as if he'd worn them for the sweatshirt relay. He stamped his feet on the worn carpet in the entryway and rubbed a wet hand over his hair, squeezing out as much water as possible before moving onto the linoleum floor. Musical notes drifted out from the sanctuary. He peeked in. A boy from his morning small group Bible study was at the piano. About twenty other kids sat scattered around the first three pews.

Brady moved up the side aisle, his wet flip-flops squeaking against the hard floor. He stopped to kick them off and saw Claire waving him over to sit with her and Hayley. She eyed his trumpet case and whispered as he sat down.

"Was that you playing at lights out last night?"

"You heard it?"

Claire nodded. "It was faint, but sound travels really well here at night. We wondered who was playing."

"Are you trying out, too?"

Claire scrunched her nose. "Yeah, Hayley talked me into singing with her."

The boy at the piano finished, and after several more campers performed, Claire and Hayley were called to the stage. They looked nervous, standing close together, microphones in hand as they waited for the recorded music to begin.

Their selection was a popular "girl" song—not one he'd listen to by choice. But their voices blended well. He liked their choreography too. And he liked Claire. Hayley was prettier, but Claire's friendliness and confidence caught his interest. Though naturally athletic, she didn't act stuck-up like some of the girl jocks at school. She was probably a couple years older than him, like Steven, which meant he didn't stand a chance with her. Still, his pulse quickened when Claire returned to sit with him after they finished their audition and Hayley left.

"I want to hear you play." She smiled, and those cute dimples appeared on her cheeks.

He was the last camper to audition. Only Claire and the two counselor judges remained. He stood alone on the stage, licked his lips, opened the spit valve and blew through the horn to clear out any moisture inside. He wiped his sweaty hands on his wet shorts and took a deep relaxing breath. His fingers bobbled the valves as he brought the horn to his lips and began to play.

The notes rang out clear and sharp. A light echo bounced off the rafters and the floor. Brady glanced at Claire. She smiled at him. The corners of his mouth curled in response, and then his mind went blank. What had he just played?

Brady stopped and pulled his horn away from his lips. "Sorry. I got lost. Can I start over?" His ears grew hot. Hopefully no one would notice them turning red.

The counselors nodded and he began again. This time he

kept his mind on the music, his gaze on the point at the back where wall, ceiling and rafters all met. He played a slow rendition of "Amazing Grace," giving it an almost mournful quality. On the second time through, he slid into a jazzy version, followed by a march, then returned to a slow, reverent tone at the end. When he finished, Claire and the counselors stood and clapped. The counselors looked at each other and both nodded.

One explained, "You weren't here at the beginning when we announced that these aren't really tryouts. Everyone who wants to perform gets to do it, but we'd like to put you at the end as our grand finale."

Claire squeezed Brady's arm as he put his horn back in its case. "You were fantastic. How'd you learn to play so well?"

Brady shrugged. "Same as everyone else, I guess. Lessons. Band. Lots of practice. I just like playing." His arm glowed warm and tingly where she touched it. He snapped the trumpet case shut and walked with her to the door. Rain still fell, but not as heavy as before.

"Guess we won't be having the picnic tonight."

She smiled. "You're lucky your cabin is close. Mine's clear across camp. Guess I'll see you in the dining hall later." She waved her fingers at him and took off for her cabin, jogging barefoot through the rain and splashing through every puddle in her path.

"Yeah, see you later," Brady breathed.

CHAPTER 9

Evening worship would start in just a few minutes, but Nurse Willie set a basin of water on the floor in front of Brady and another one in front of Steven. "Put your feet in there and use this soap to wash 'em good. Be sure you get between your toes and all the way up to your knees."

"But I'm not itching." Brady hated the thought of being late in case Claire was waiting for them.

Willie looked down her nose at him. "Not yet, but you'll thank me later. Wash your sandals too. Get all that plant residue off."

Brady sat next to Steven in one of the clinic's molded plastic chairs and grumbled to himself. What an idiot he was, taking Steven through the woods to search out the other team's flag. He'd never seen poison ivy before. A poster on the wall showed pictures of venomous snakes and dangerous plants. Even after studying it, Brady wouldn't have recognized the stuff among all the other leafy plants they'd stumbled through. Not long after the flag was finally captured, Steven's ankle looked sunburned, and he complained that it itched like crazy.

Brady wrinkled his nose at the clinic's antiseptic smell. It reminded him of the doctor's office and shots. The clinic wasn't much bigger than his bedroom at home. A cot with a thin vinyl mattress took up most of the opposite wall. An adjacent door opened onto a small bathroom. White cupboards and drawers likely held bandages and medical supplies, and two other yellowed posters on the wall illustrated the inner workings of knees and ears.

"Okay, I'm finished." He held his dripping hands over the tub.

Willie handed towels to him and Steven. "Dry your feet and hands with these. When you're finished, Brady can take the tubs and dump the water into the toilet."

While Brady cleaned up, she examined Steven's ankle. "Most people don't react this quickly, but it's not unheard of. Try not to scratch it. I'd give you an antihistamine but you might fall asleep in the middle of Zeke's talk. For now, let's do this." She sprayed his ankle and Steven let out a happy sigh. "Come back after evening worship and I'll give you the antihistamine. You'll need it if you want to sleep tonight."

Willie took the empty tubs from Brady, and clicked her tongue as he and Steven slipped their feet into flip- flops. The colorful lures on her hat swayed as she shook her head. "Better shoes would've protected you from the poison ivy. I'll never understand why you kids wear those flimsy things."

Brady made a mental note to remember that the next time he decided to run around in the woods.

Willie turned off the clinic light and followed them through the entryway. "I'm going out to keep the fish company, but I'll be back by the time you need me." She stopped at a closet and pulled out a life jacket, canoe paddle, fishing pole and tackle box.

Steven pushed open the outside door. "Can we go fishing too?"

Willie frowned at them as she slipped the life jacket on. "And miss evening worship? You know the answer to that question."

Steven laughed. "Yeah I do, but it never hurts to ask."

Willie ushered them out of the clinic and locked the door. "You boys hurry now, or you'll be late."

Brady led Steven along a shortcut to the chapel. They arrived with little time to spare. Campers swarmed the front rows, forcing them to sit farther back. Before he sat down, Brady searched the crowd for a glimpse of Claire. Instead, he spotted someone else and nudged Steven's knee.

"Guess who's sitting up front?"

A slow smile spread over Steven's face. "Taylor?"

"Yep."

"Ha-ha. Sweet punishment."

Brady's gaze swept across each row from one side to the other until he found Claire. She sat a couple rows up on the other side of the aisle, with Hayley next to her. She turned and caught him watching her, then stood and squeezed past the other girls to cross the aisle.

She tapped Steven's shoulder. "Did Brady tell you we're both in the talent show?"

"Yeah, you and Hayley. Since when do you dance?"

"I don't. It's just a few moves that Hayley talked me into." She smiled at Brady. "Will your parents be here for the show?"

Her question knocked the wind out of him. "No. Why?"

"It's sort of a tradition," Steven explained. "If you're in the talent show, your parents can come and watch. Zeke lets them stay over Friday night in the guesthouse, so they can take you home on Saturday. But you don't have to invite them."

Claire clucked. "Are you kidding? If I sang as well as you play, my mom would kill me if I didn't invite her." She glanced at the band as they started their opening song. "Uh-oh, I'd better get back. Talk to you later."

Brady stood to sing with the rest of the campers, but no words came out of his mouth. His mind raced from one thought to another, like a deflating balloon zooming crazily around the room. Did everyone invite their parents? How many of them came? Would he be the only one with no parents to clap for him? Should he try inviting Mom?

The talent show was Friday, the same day as his birthday. He hadn't told anyone yet and probably wouldn't. That way, if no one wished him happy birthday, he wouldn't be disappointed. He'd learned not to expect anything from his dad, but would Mom remember? A card, at least? How could he find out what he had done to make her so angry? Whatever it was, he'd fix it. He'd change.

The music stopped and Brady sat down, shoving the troubling thoughts from his mind as Zeke took the stage.

With Bible in hand, Zeke said, "Genesis tells us that every evening, God walked through the Garden with Adam and Eve." His bushy eyebrows shot up and his jaw dropped. "Can you imagine walking around the block with God? Every day? What would you talk about? Sports? Music? Gardening? Religion? The Bible doesn't tell us what they talked about, but it does say those evening walks came to an abrupt end when Adam and Eve disobeyed God's command. They ate fruit from the forbidden tree."

Brady remembered that story from long ago when his family went to church. When he still had a family.

"All of you have disobeyed your parents at some time or other, right?" Zeke asked. "They told you not to hang around with so-and-so, or be home by a certain time. 'Do this. Don't do that.' But you went ahead and did it anyway. Then you felt a little guilty and didn't want them to find out, so you tried to hide it."

Zeke paced the stage. "Adam and Eve felt guilty too. Their disobedience ripped apart their relationship with God." He picked up a shirt and held it so everyone could see.

Brady leaned over and whispered to Steven. "He's holding up a torn blue shirt and sticking his fingers through the hole."

"When you tear your favorite shirt or pants," Zeke continued, "it creates a hole. Your mom might try patching it, but it's never the same. Why? Because those threads that were woven together are broken." He wadded the shirt up and tossed it aside, then moved to his easel and drew some ragged marks on the paper. "What do you end up doing with those favorite jeans or shirt that gets torn?"

Someone in the audience shouted, "Wear 'em."

Zeke's sketching hand froze, and he knocked his head against the paper. His shoulders shook with laughter. "Okay. You're right. With the jeans, you'd poke more holes in them and sell them for a bunch of money. But what about your favorite shirt?" He resumed sketching. "You'd probably quit wearing it. Eventually you'd throw it out. That's what happened to Adam and Eve. When the fabric of their relationship with God was torn, God forced them out of the Garden, out of their home."

Brady sat up straight. This was sounding familiar. God told Adam and Eve he didn't want them living there anymore.

But unlike him, Adam and Eve knew what they'd done wrong. He had no clue, except that Mom didn't smile anymore, not like she used to.

Mom had been so excited marrying Richard. "You'll finally have a dad," she'd told him. "With both of us working, we'll have enough money to watch movies at the theater and go out for pizza. Maybe we can even get you a car when you turn sixteen."

But Richard didn't have any more time for him than Dad did. Brady would rather make do without the movies and pizza, even the car, if it would bring back Mom's smile.

Still, should he invite her to the talent show? It would give him an excuse to call her. *Maybe she's changed her mind. Maybe I can still live with her and Richard.* The tone of her voice when she left on Sunday didn't give him much hope. He dreaded hearing that again. Did she really mean what she'd said? Would he survive if she said yes, she really meant it?

Nope, calling wasn't worth the risk.

Steven bumped his arm. "You haven't told me what Zeke's drawing."

He'd been so caught up in his own thoughts he'd missed most of Zeke's talk. The drawing had taken shape without him really seeing it. "Looks like Jesus," he whispered. "Mainly his head with a piece of the cross sticking up in back."

Brady bowed his head with the rest of the campers as Zeke led the final prayer. Much of the message had escaped him, but the part he'd heard hit home.

What else changed for Adam and Eve? Did they miss talking with God, hearing His voice? Were they afraid of what He might say the next time he spoke? Did they ever wonder if God still loved them?

***

Brady finished his "lights-out lullaby," as Steven called it. Crickets chirruped in the woods and moths batted themselves against the light outside the door.

Matt came out of the cabin and sat down. "I'm glad you auditioned for the talent show."

Brady walked over and lifted a foot onto the step. "Are we supposed to invite our parents?"

"You can, but you don't have to. Are you thinking about your mom?"

Brady nodded. "She probably wouldn't come anyway."

Matt reached out and tapped Brady's knee. "Are you doing okay here?"

He nodded again, and blinked rapidly as his eyes stung with tears.

Matt jerked his head toward the cabin and whispered, "Has Taylor given you any more trouble?" Brady shook his head. "If he does, you need to tell me."

Brady stepped up and reached for the screen door but stopped short of opening it. "Can I ask you something?"

"Sure."

"Did God still love Adam and Eve after he kicked them out of the Garden?"

"Absolutely. God never stopped loving them. Getting kicked out of the Garden sounds like punishment to us, but it might have been an act of love."

Brady frowned. "Love? How?"

Matt leaned back and looked up at him. "They ate from the Tree of Knowledge of Good and Evil, but Genesis tells of another tree in the Garden called the Tree of Life. Scholars think that eating from it kept you physically alive forever. In the perfect Garden of Eden, that was a good thing. But when Adam and Eve disobeyed, they suddenly knew what evil was.

God never intended for them to live forever with such horrible knowledge. The Bible says God removed them from the Garden so they wouldn't eat from the Tree of Life and live forever with the knowledge of sin and evil."

Brady toyed with the trumpet's mouthpiece, pulling it out, in, out, in. "So He kicked them out, but He did still love them. Right?"

Matt gazed at him, a look of pity on his face. Brady hated that. "You're right. He never stopped loving them, just like He never stops loving us."

Brady started to open the door, but Matt stopped him.

"Listen, I don't know what made your mom say and do what she did. But I know for sure that God loves you more than you could ever imagine. Over and over in the Bible, He says, 'I will never leave you or desert you.' Do you trust Him?"

Brady shrugged. "I...I don't know."

"I like your honesty." Matt stood and placed a hand on his shoulder. "I'm praying that by the end of the week, you'll know beyond any doubt that you can trust His love for you, no matter what happens." He pulled open the screen door. "G'night."

Brady put his trumpet away and climbed to the top bunk. Steven was already asleep, probably from the medicine Willie gave him. Brady took a deep breath and let it out slowly, willing his body to relax. If he decided to invite his mom, he'd need to call her no later than Thursday. Making that decision would be easier if he had time to play his trumpet, time to think and sort things out. Tomorrow, he'd ask Matt where he could practice without being interrupted.

Brady closed his eyes. Did he trust God? How can you trust something you can't see, especially when the people and things you can see let you down? Would God answer Matt's prayer? *I hope so. It'd be nice to have someone in my life that would never leave.*

CHAPTER 10

Morning sunshine warmed Brady's shoulders as he sat with his study group around the campfire pit. A hundred yards away, beyond the steep drop-off, the lake reflected a deeper shade of the blue sky above. Bird songs mixed with the gentle lapping of waves at the shore, and a light fishy smell mingled with the earthy scent of moist ground after yesterday's rain.

Bethany, the small group leader, recapped the story of Jonah and asked, "Who can tell me how this story demonstrates God's love and care for his people?"

Brady avoided eye contact with her and squirmed as dampness from the log he was sitting on seeped through his shorts. He tugged the cloth away from his skin, glancing around to make sure no one else noticed. A borrowed Bible balanced on his lap, and he tried to figure out how Mom decided on this camp. Did the fact that it was a church camp matter to her, or was it just the first one she found?

Bethany waved her hand. "Hello? Anybody awake this morning?"

One of the girls fluttered her hand in the air before she answered. He'd seen her with Claire in chapel last night so they were probably in the same cabin.

"Hey!" One of the boys pointed to his Bible. "It says here the fish vomited Jonah onto dry land."

"Eeuw!" The girls scrunched their noses.

Bethany rolled her eyes. "Yeah, it's gross, but let's think about situations we've been in that seemed hopeless. Did it feel like God was in control?"

Brady closed his eyes and tipped his head back, letting the sun bathe his face. If God was in control, He was doing a lousy job. He commanded a fish to swallow Jonah; was it that much harder to keep Mom and Dad together? And what about last night's lesson? Couldn't God have kept Adam and Eve from eating that fruit? Matt said God removed them from the Garden because He loved them. But getting kicked out of your home sure doesn't feel like love.

Brady let his mind wander. Should he invite Mom to the talent show? Maybe she'd come if he asked it as a favor for his birthday. She'd always made a big deal over his birthday.

Bethany interrupted his thoughts. "Brady, don't fall asleep on me."

His eyes popped open. "I'm awake."

"Good." She smiled at him. "Have you ever felt hopeless, like God wasn't in control?"

Now.

He shrugged. "Maybe."

"Let's all look at Jonah's prayer in chapter two." She waited until everyone found the right page. "He talks about waves and breakers covering him, sinking deep down to the roots of the mountains, seaweed wrapped around his head. Sounds like someone who's drowning. He might have been minutes away from death. Maybe only seconds."

Bethany leaned forward. "Sometimes, God allows things to get out of control in our lives to get our attention. If life is fine and nothing's bothering us, why do we need God? We can handle life all by ourselves, right? But if you're drowning, you can't save yourself. You focus totally on whatever you need to survive. God is like a life preserver. He helps us survive when we're drowning. But the time to put on the life preserver is before you get in the boat, right? You can't wait until you're drowning."

That's for sure. After yesterday, he'd always make sure his life jacket was fastened. In the distance, a motorboat chugged across the lake and pulled up beside an old boathouse that leaned to the side, as if tired of standing.

The girl from Claire's cabin giggled. She read a note from her friend sitting next to her, then scribbled an answer and passed it back. Her eyes met Brady's and she flashed him a guilty grin.

At last, Bethany dismissed them and Brady headed for the dining hall to meet Steven. Behind him, the girls chattered, and Claire's name drew his attention. He shortened his stride to better hear the conversation.

One of the girls giggled. "He likes her?"

"Can't you tell?"

"But she doesn't like him, does she?"

"Shhhh! Not so loud. No way. She says he acts like he's back in fourth grade." The girls veered off toward their cabin.

Were they talking about him? He thought he'd done a pretty good job of hiding his feelings for Claire. But if they weren't talking about him, why all the shushing? It had to be him. His stomach twisted at the idea that Claire thought he was immature, childish.

How stupid of him to think a girl like Claire might notice him. Still, she didn't seem like the kind of girl who'd say such things. Or was she? The image of her victory dance in the sand came to mind, along with the way she rubbed their win in Taylor's face. Brady's steps grew heavy and slow as he approached the corner of the dining hall where Steven waited for him.

"Brady? Is that you?" Steven cocked an ear in Brady's direction.

"Yeah." Brady forced an evenness to his voice.

"Everything okay?"

"Just great. You ready to go?"

"You don't sound just great."

"I'm fine. Okay?" This time, he couldn't hide the irritation in his voice. He wanted to be alone, to vent his frustration and anger through his trumpet. Instead, he nudged Steven's arm with his elbow. "Let's go see what we're doing for Rec today."

They walked to the side of the Snack Shack, and Brady studied the announcement board. "Volleyball today. You can't do that, can you?"

Steven shook his head, but spoke with excitement. "Nope. Maybe Willie can take me fishing again."

Brady's mood deteriorated even further. He'd counted on Steven's presence the next time he faced Claire. Without Steven around as a distraction, he'd have to pretend friendship with her, and that wouldn't be easy. "Let's go back to the cabin and drop off our Bibles before lunch."

"Okay. Maybe this time, I can talk Zeke into letting you come fishing too." Steven took hold of Brady's elbow and they started for the cabin.

At least Steven could be trusted. He always took Brady's side, even if it meant suffering the same abuse. *And speaking of abuse...*

Taylor strolled toward them with two girls, one on each side. He said something, and the girls' laughter sounded mocking.

Brady made an effort to follow Steven's advice and ignore them. He moved to the side, giving them wide passage.

"Hey, losers," Taylor taunted. "Is it true what I heard–that your mothers sent you to camp to get rid of you for a week?"

One of the girls gasped. "Taylor, that's so mean." The words were barely out of her mouth before she started to giggle. The other girl joined in.

Brady's ears burned. His jaw hardened as the heat traveled from his ears to his neck, down into his shoulders and his arms.

"Ignore him," Steven said, squeezing Brady's elbow. He tugged sideways. "Just keep walking."

Steven's voice sounded distant, as if he were a hundred yards away, while Taylor's voice replayed loud and clear in Brady's mind. He smacked his Bible against Steven's stomach.

"Hang onto this." Wrenching his elbow away, he darted toward Taylor and leaped onto his back, wrapping an arm around his neck. Anger coursed through his body. He tightened his hold.

The girls screamed. Taylor bent over, leaned to one side and spun around. Brady held on, even when Taylor dropped to the ground, pinning him beneath his back. Trapped, Brady clamped his legs around Taylor's hips. He clenched his jaw tight, barely noticing Steven's calls.

Taylor dug his fingernails into Brady's arm, raking the

flesh and threatening to loosen his stranglehold. But resistance only fueled Brady's anger, and he squeezed even tighter around Taylor's throat.

His other fist pummeled Taylor's chest and ribs, the side of his head, and any other place he could reach.

Taylor slammed his head backward against Brady's forehead. Stars swirled against black, and he struggled to maintain his grip as Taylor rolled to the side, squirming first one way then another.

A gathering crowd shouted and screamed, but he paid no attention until his fist was halted in mid-punch. Someone wrenched his arm from Taylor's neck, allowing Taylor to scramble away. Yanked upright, Brady tried one last swing but found his wrist in a solid grip.

"Stop it, now!" Matt jerked him backward, and planted one hand on Taylor's chest, gathering his shirt in a tight fist to keep him from lunging at Brady. "Both of you, take some deep breaths and calm down."

Brady's chest was already heaving. He wiped the corners of his mouth with his wrist. Blood oozed from his forearm where Taylor had scratched him.

"All right." Matt's grip barely relaxed. "Who wants to start explaining?"

"I didn't do anything," Taylor protested. "I was just walking along, minding my own business. He jumped me from behind and pulled me to the ground. I was trying to get away."

"He's right." One of the girls spoke up. "All of a sudden, this kid jumped him from behind."

Matt looked at Brady. "Is that true?"

"No, they're lying." Steven felt his way through the crowd. "He wasn't just minding his business. You know the kind of things he says. That's what started it."

"Okay, all of you to Zeke's office. Girls, you too. Let's go." Matt jerked his head toward the building, but warned Taylor, "You keep your mouth closed. Not one word." Before he let go of Brady's arm, he leaned in nose to nose. "You don't touch Taylor. Understand? Don't even breathe in his direction." Matt guided Steven and spoke over his shoulder to the crowd. "The rest of you need to find something better to do."

Brady kept his distance from Taylor as Matt ushered them into Zeke's office and explained why they were there. Taylor slumped into an armchair positioned in front of the desk.

"On your feet, son." Zeke's voice was low and controlled. "No one sits until we sort this out." His eyes held a stern look as he studied them over the top of his glasses.

Brady met Zeke's gaze only briefly. If he wasn't so angry, he might feel a tiny bit ashamed. Maybe.

Zeke began the investigation. "What started all this?"

Taylor jabbed a finger at Brady. "He started it. The girls and I were just walking along when this loser comes up behind and tries to strangle me. Isn't that right?" He looked at the girls who exchanged glances, but remained silent.

"No, it's not right," Steven said. "Brady and I were walking to the cabin. I'm not sure exactly where Taylor was, but he's the one who started it. He's always talking trash, and he said our moms probably sent us here so they could be rid of us for the week. After that, Brady tore away from me, and I heard them fighting."

Zeke took off his glasses and peered at Brady. "I don't put up with fights here at Rustic Knoll. I could send you home."

Good luck. Mom'll probably send me back.

Hopefully Zeke wouldn't insist on an apology. He wasn't sorry. Adrenaline still coursed through his body, but he took a deep breath and exhaled slowly as his breathing returned to normal.

Zeke shifted his attention to Taylor. "What do you have to say for yourself?"

"I was just teasing." Taylor slid his hands into his armpits and clamped his arms down tight. "The kid can't even take a joke. All of a sudden, he's choking me. Can't I defend myself?"

Zeke's lips pressed into a thin line as he put his glasses back on. "Matt, I'd like you to stay. Ladies and Steven, you three may go."

"Do I have to?" Steven asked.

Zeke glanced at him over his glasses. "You can wait outside if you like."

The girls hurried out. Matt took Steven into the hallway, then returned and closed the door behind him. He leaned against a wall as Zeke motioned Brady and Taylor to sit down. Brady took the closest armchair, shuffling it away from Taylor.

Zeke picked up a pen, toying with it as he leaned back in his chair. "Taylor, I didn't expect to see you back in my office so soon. First you tip over a canoe, and now a fight. Do you have something against Brady and Steven?"

Taylor's shoulders hunched together. "They're just easy to tease." He waited for Zeke's response, his knee bobbing up and down. In the silence, he added, "I'm here 'cuz my mom wanted me out of her hair. What's the big deal?"

Brady threw him a side-glance, then looked away and muttered, "I don't blame her."

Zeke frowned at him, and he clamped his lips tight to keep from saying anything else.

The director lifted his Bible from the desk and paged

through it. "So, you think the things you say don't matter." He got up and handed the open Bible to Taylor. "Read James 3:6. Out loud, please."

Taylor's lips moved as his finger traced the lines on the page. "'The tongue also is a fire, a world of evil among the parts of the body. It corrupts the whole person, sets the whole course of his life on fire, and is itself set on fire by hell.'"

Brady stifled a grin at the scowl on Taylor's face.

"It's not that bad," Taylor mumbled.

"No? Try Matthew 12:36." Zeke settled back in his chair.

Taylor flipped the pages and ran his finger down until he found the verse. "But I tell you that men will have to give account on the day of judgment for every careless word they have spoken."

"Those are Jesus' very words, Taylor. God does care about the things we say, enough to hold us accountable."

Taylor made a sour face and closed the Bible.

"Not so fast." Zeke pointed to the closed book. "Ephesians 4:29."

Taylor leaned an elbow on one knee and balanced the Bible on the other. He flipped pages back and forth until Matt helped him find the verse. "Do not let any unwholesome talk come out of your mouths, but only what is helpful for building others up according to their needs, that it may benefit those who listen."

"'That it may benefit those who listen.' Think about that for a few minutes." He pulled another Bible off the shelf behind his desk, and held it out to Brady. "First Peter, chapter three, verse nine."

Brady took the Bible, and made several passes through the whole book. "Where is it?"

Matt leaned down and flipped pages until they came to

First Peter. Brady turned another page to the third chapter and put his finger on verse nine. He glanced at Zeke and read out loud. "Do not repay evil with evil or insult with insult, but with blessing, because to this you were called so that you may inherit a blessing."

Zeke nodded. "Now, turn back a few pages to Ephesians, chapter four. Read verse 32."

With Matt's help again, Brady found the spot. "Be kind and compassionate to one another, forgiving each other, just as in Christ God forgave you."

Fat chance.

Zeke leaned forward, his elbows on the desk. "Brady, look at that verse again. Tell me, does it say to bless people because they deserve it? Are we supposed to forgive others only when they apologize?"

It was obvious where this was going, but he shook his head anyway.

Zeke pressed his point. "Why does it say to forgive people?"

"Because God forgave us."

"That's right. Forgiveness doesn't mean that the other person is right, or that what they said or did is okay. It's still wrong. But when you forgive someone, you give up your right to revenge, and you leave the punishment in God's hands. Does that make sense?"

Brady looked to Matt, then back at Zeke. "Are you saying I have to forgive him for all the evil stuff he's said and for dumping us out of the canoe?"

A corner of Zeke's mouth pulled up as he glanced at Matt. "That's exactly what I'm saying. And your expression tells me you're not quite ready for that. So I'm going to help you out. Turn to Luke 6:28 and read that for me."

Brady found Luke quickly and read the verse to himself first, then out loud. "Bless those who curse you, pray for those who mistreat you."

"I think that's an appropriate verse to apply in this situation. So," Zeke clapped his hands together, "Taylor, your assignment is to memorize Ephesians 4:29. You will stay here in my office until you can say it out loud, word for word. Brady, you will memorize Luke 6:28. Matt, you will accompany Brady back to the cabin where he's to stay until I decide whether or not to send him home." His gaze swept from Brady to Taylor and back again. "Both of you will be prepared to recite your verse for me every time I see you between now and the time you leave Rustic Knoll. Understood?"

"What about lunch?" Taylor rubbed his nose with his fist.

Zeke's mustache twitched. "I suggest you start memorizing now so you'll have time to get something to eat. Matt, you can get a tray for Brady since he'll have to stay in the cabin."

Brady laid the Bible on Zeke's desk and tried to imagine his mom's reaction if Zeke sent him home. He knew what she'd have done before, but now? He had no clue.

CHAPTER 11

Brady stormed out of Zeke's office with Matt on his heels.

Steven jumped to his feet. "What happened? I bet you have to memorize a Bible verse, don't you?"

Brady brushed past him. Even though Steven had defended him, he didn't want to talk about it.

Matt filled in the details. "He's on cabin detention. I have to make sure he gets there. You coming, or do you want to go to lunch?"

"I'm with Brady."

Brady didn't wait for them. He couldn't get to the cabin fast enough, especially when he spotted Claire, Hayley, and another girl coming toward them. He ducked his head, but Claire left the others and jogged over.

"Hey, where are you going? Lunch is that way." She pointed to the dining hall, but when no one responded her dimples disappeared with her smile, and her brows scrunched together. "You guys look serious. Did something happen?"

Brady kept his gaze trained on the ground.

Matt simply waved as they hurried past. "Have a good lunch."

"Wait! What's going on? Tell me."

Brady quickened his pace. She'd find out soon enough. At least he didn't have to worry about seeing her at volleyball. He squeezed his hands into fists, then opened them and stretched his fingers–a trick he'd learned at music contests to release tension.

The screen door creaked when Matt pulled it open then slammed shut behind them.

Brady climbed up on his bunk and flipped onto his back. Matt stopped off at his room while Steven continued on, counting beds until he reached Brady's. He stood in the aisle, arms hanging limp at his sides and eyebrows furrowed over his dark glasses.

"What happened, Brady?"

"I don't want to talk about it." He narrowed his eyes until all he could see was a knothole in the ceiling above his head.

Steven moved closer. "I heard what Taylor said, but why'd you go after him? I mean, was it worth fighting…"

"I said I don't want to talk. Just shut up about it, okay?" Brady threw himself onto his stomach, cradled the pillow in his arms and buried his face.

Why *did* he go after Taylor? He'd never been in a fight before, much less started one. Plenty of times, he'd imagined the satisfaction of smashing Taylor's face, but he never actually considered doing it. It wasn't something he'd planned. He couldn't even recall the thought that propelled him onto Taylor's back. He only remembered— clearly—what was said. Maybe if it hadn't been so close to the truth, he'd have let it pass.

The screen door screeched and slammed, and Dillon entered the bunkroom. "Where's Brady? I heard he smacked Taylor."

Brady pushed his face deeper into the pillow, turning his head to the side to breathe. Something jarred the bunk, and he peeked under his arm to see what it was.

Steven blocked Dillon's path. "He doesn't want to talk about it. Leave him alone."

"Did he really fight Taylor?" Dillon's walking cast clunked against the floor as he moved around Steven to the other side of the bunk. He was breathing hard, as if he'd hurried to get there.

Steven moved in the direction of his voice. "Yeah, but..."

"Brady, you're a beast!" Dillon laughed and slapped Brady on the back. "Man, I never guessed you'd be the one to put him in his place." He pressed Brady's shoulder, trying to turn him over.

Brady shrugged his hand away.

"Come on, Brady, you're awesome. Let's see your battle scars."

"Leave me alone!" Brady swung his pillow sideways, catching Dillon on the side of his head and knocking him off-balance.

"Whoa! Nice swing." Dillon laughed as he steadied himself.

Brady hugged the pillow again, hiding as best he could.

"Do what he says, Dillon. Leave him alone." Matt spoke low and commanding.

"Okay, okay. But Brady, you can play on my team anytime, y'hear?"

In the sliver of space between the pillow and his arm,

Brady glimpsed Dillon holding out his fists, thumbs pointing up. His laughter left the cabin with him, and Matt came to stand in Dillon's spot.

"I'm going to get some lunch. You want me to bring a tray back for you?"

"How long is he on cabin detention?" Steven asked.

"Until Zeke decides whether or not to send him home." Matt laid a hand on Brady's shoulder. "Are you hungry?"

Brady came out of hiding and raised himself up on one elbow. "I guess so."

"Steven, you want to come with me?"

"I'd rather stay here."

Brady sat up. "Go ahead. You don't have to babysit me."

Steven shook his head. "I want to stay. Can you bring a tray for me, too?"

"Your choice. I'll be back in a little bit." Matt left, the screen door slamming behind him.

As if on cue, Steven's questions began. "Hey, Brady?"

How many times did he have to tell him? "I said I don't want...."

"It's not about the fight." Steven leaned his shoulder against Brady's bunk. "If Zeke sends you home, where will you go?"

Brady lay back down on his side, and hugged the pillow to his chest. "There's no way I'm living with my dad. If Mom doesn't want me...I don't know. Maybe I'll run away and live on my own somewhere."

Steven felt for the bed behind him and sank onto it. "Aw, that's not a good idea." His brow puckered. "Your mom's serious? I mean, she wasn't just having a bad day? Could she change her mind?"

Brady frowned and pulled the pillow a little tighter. "Even

114

if she did, I don't think Richard wants me around."

"Richard?"

"My stepdad. I think it was his idea for me to live with my dad."

"Are you going to invite them to the talent show?"

Brady rolled onto his back. "Mom wouldn't come."

"How do you know?" Steven jumped up, hands reaching out until they found the bed frame. He stepped onto the bottom bunk and stood close to where Brady lay. "What if you call your mom and say you're sorry for whatever, then invite her to the talent show because you're playing the grand finale."

Brady moved his head from side to side. "She's heard me play before. Why would she come all the way up here to listen to something she's heard at home?"

"Because she's your mom. You gotta try. If she comes, it's your chance to talk her out of sending you to your dad."

Brady pushed up onto his elbow. "It won't work. Besides, I may not be here for the talent show. Remember?"

"Oh, yeah." Steven stepped down to the floor and backed away. "Well, if Zeke doesn't send you home, promise you'll invite her."

Brady lay back down and tucked his hands beneath his head. What did he have to lose?

"Yeah, sure. Whatever."

***

Matt returned with a lunch tray and enough food for both Brady and Steven. His presence in the bunkroom squelched any talk of the fight as other boys trickled in from lunch.

Brady caught their curious glances, an occasional smirk, and a secret thumbs up. When Taylor walked in, an unnatural quiet descended on the room.

Matt prodded everyone to hurry to Rec activities,

assigning Chris to help Steven. After everyone left, he hoisted himself onto the bunk next to Brady's and sat with his legs hanging over the side.

Was he staying in the cabin? Didn't he need to supervise Rec activities? Brady avoided eye contact, thumbing through pages of the Bible he'd thrust at Steven earlier. He found his assigned memory verse and mouthed the words.

"It helps if you say it out loud," Matt said. "Try it."

"'Bless those who curse you.'" Brady peeked at his Bible. "'And pray for those who mistreat you.'"

"Can you do that?"

Brady blew air through his lips. "Maybe, if I wanted to."

Matt shook his head. "It doesn't say to do it if you want to. Nobody wants to pray for people who act like jerks. Okay, rather than asking if you *can* do it, let me ask, *will* you do it?"

Brady hunched one shoulder.

One of Matt's flip-flops fell to the floor. He kicked off the other one, pulled his legs up and crossed them. "I bet you didn't feel like getting out of bed this morning. Would've been nice to sleep in, huh? But you got up, even though you didn't want to. We do a lot of things we don't want to. Which proves we can pray for someone we don't like, someone we don't want to pray for."

Brady's finger played with the pages of his Bible. "But if I don't really mean it, what good is it?"

"The good comes from our obedience. It's nice if the feelings come with it, but God cares more about our actions than our feelings. And it's okay to be honest. He knows how you feel anyway, so tell him you don't want to pray for Taylor, that you're only doing it because He told you to."

Matt's analogy made sense. But praying for Taylor simply didn't fit into his imagination. "What am I supposed to say? I mean, God probably wouldn't like it if I asked him to strike Taylor with lightning or something."

"No, probably not." Matt chuckled. "At least you'd be honest. How about if I say a prayer first?"

Matt folded his hands and bowed his head. "Jesus, you know exactly what Brady is going through with Taylor. You suffered insults and the horrible things people said about you when you walked this earth. Thank you for sharing in our problems and suffering. Lord, I ask you to bless Taylor. Whatever is going on in his life that makes him act the way he does, I pray that you would change him from the inside out. And I ask you to give Brady the strength and ability to deal with Taylor's irritating habits. Amen."

Brady couldn't bring himself to join Matt's prayer. He closed his eyes and opened them slowly, hoping Matt wouldn't know he'd been watching him rather than praying with him.

Matt opened his eyes and frowned. "That sounded more complicated than I wanted. Just ask God to bless Taylor in whatever way He chooses. I know you can say those words, so I won't make you pray out loud. But work on it, okay? What's your verse?"

Brady checked his Bible again before reciting it. "'Bless those who curse you. Pray for those who mistreat you.'"

"Good job." Matt jumped down from the bunk and slid his feet into his sandals. "I probably should head out to Rec. You want your trumpet?"

"Yeah!" Brady scrambled down from his bunk and retrieved his horn from Matt's room.

Matt stopped him before he left. "Listen, I understand why you jumped Taylor. Not saying it's right, but I understand. I've been in your shoes and believe me, you don't have to fight anyone. I'm here for you, okay? Anytime you need me. And I'm praying that God heals every wound that people have left in your life so you can honestly pray for Taylor, and for your mom, too."

He delivered a light punch to Brady's shoulder. "Hey, I know it's not cool for guys to talk about stuff that's bothering them. Come punch me in the arm or something and I'll know you want to talk. Deal?"

Brady nodded and made a quick escape back to the bunkroom. Matt called a good-bye as he left, and the tension in Brady's shoulders dissolved. He'd have the cabin to himself with time to play his trumpet. Not what he considered punishment, but he'd never admit that to Zeke.

CHAPTER 12

An hour later, Steven hobbled into the cabin and sank onto his bed.

Brady quit playing his horn long enough to ask, "What happened?"

"Tandem bike ride with Ryan." He lifted his feet onto the bed and massaged his legs. "Are you bored yet?"

Brady laid his trumpet aside. "Not yet. Been playing my horn."

Chris ran in, letting the screen door slam. "Lucky you guys didn't have to play volleyball. We lost all three games. It was bad." He grabbed a towel off the end of his bed and wiped the sweat from his face. "Steven, Claire said to meet her down at the beach."

"Can't. I'm staying here."

Brady objected. "Go swim if you want. I don't need a babysitter." He blew the spit out of his trumpet, wiped off the fingerprints and laid it in the case.

Steven dropped his feet to the floor. "I'm not babysitting you. Just figured I'd keep you company. I'd hate being here all afternoon by myself."

"I'm fine." Brady slid the trumpet under Steven's bed and climbed up to his top bunk. Which was worse, being alone or listening to Steven's chatter all afternoon? Maybe Zeke would come by and either release him or send him home.

Chris grabbed his swim trunks and headed for the bathroom. "If you're going to the beach, I'm leaving as soon as I change."

The odor of sweaty bodies and loud voices filled the cabin as more boys returned from Rec. Steven felt for his swim trunks hanging over the clothes bar in the open closet. "What if Taylor comes in?"

Brady wrinkled his nose. "I'll be okay. Go on." Right now, he'd rather face Taylor than Claire. He was glad he wasn't going with Steven. But after his friends left, resentment set in. He suddenly hated this confinement.

He gazed around the room, trying to think of something to do when Taylor strutted into the bunkroom. Their eyes locked. The hostility in Taylor's gaze mirrored Brady's lingering anger. Taylor's mouth opened, his lip pulling up into a sneer.

"Get what you need, Taylor." Matt spoke from the doorway. He crossed his arms over his chest. "You've got two minutes to get your stuff and go."

Taylor glanced back toward Matt and threw one more look of challenge at Brady before grabbing a ball cap and heading out. Matt shot Brady a warning look and followed Taylor out the door.

Brady blew out a deep breath and lay back on his bed. What were the words Matt said to pray? *Dear God, Please bless Taylor in whatever way he wants.* That didn't sound right, but it was the best he could do at the moment.

***

The boys trickled back to the cabin in twos and threes, then left again when it was time for supper. Brady still waited for word from Zeke, while Steven chattered on about every little thing that had happened outside the cabin that afternoon.

"Steven, let's go to supper." Matt walked over to his bunk.

"Can't I stay with Brady?"

"We'll bring a tray back for him. Come on." He guided Steven out. The screen door slammed and the cabin fell silent again.

Brady took out his trumpet and ran through a couple songs he'd memorized. Restless, he got up and walked around while playing. At an open window, he stopped and played his talent show selection to an imaginary audience. The screen door's creak alerted him to someone's presence, but he ignored it until he'd finished his performance. He turned and saw Zeke leaning against the doorframe.

"Sorry! I didn't know it was you. I would've quit playing."

Zeke stepped into the bunkroom. "I'm glad you didn't. Now I understand what everyone's talking about. Where'd you learn to play like that?"

Brady shrugged. "I don't know. I just like doing it." His fingers mashed the valve keys up and down.

"Have a seat." Zeke motioned him to sit on the nearest bed and sat down opposite him. He leaned forward, resting his elbows on his knees. "First, let me hear you say your verse."

Brady searched his memory for the starting word. It was an odd one, not the kind he normally used. Grace? No. Brace?

121

B–bless! "Bless those who curse you. Pray for those who mistreat you."

The corners of Zeke's mouth hid beneath his white mustache when he smiled. "Good. And Matt says you're working on doing what it says."

"I did pray for Taylor." Once. That was honest. Twice if Matt's prayer was included, but since he hadn't closed his eyes, it probably didn't count.

Zeke sat up straight. "I'm glad to hear that. I've talked with Taylor some more about the teasing. He understands there's to be no more. And I've decided not to send you home, provided there's no more fighting."

Brady's shoulders relaxed, and his breath came out in a whoosh. "It won't happen again. I promise." He laid the trumpet on the bed. "Do I still have to stay in the cabin?"

"After supper, you may leave. I assume someone's bringing you a tray?"

He nodded. "Matt and Steven said they would."

"All right then." Zeke's fingers tapped together between his knees. He appeared to study something underneath the bed. "Matt tells me things at home are not the way you'd like them. That might explain why you went after Taylor, but it doesn't justify it. It's important to learn how to express your anger in acceptable ways, not by fighting. Do you understand?"

"Yes, sir." Brady didn't want to go over all this again. He reached for his horn and twisted the mouthpiece round and round.

"If something bothers you so much you feel out of control, I hope you'll come talk to me or Matt or any of the counselors. That's why we're here. My goal is that everyone who comes to Rustic Knoll takes something home with them." He caught Brady's eye and winked. "Black eyes don't count."

Brady couldn't keep the corners of his mouth from turning up.

Zeke stood to go. "I'll leave you to your practice." He walked to the doorway and turned around. "What was that verse again?"

"Bless those who curse you. Pray for those who mistreat you." Brady rattled it off with ease this time.

Zeke clicked his tongue and winked. "That's it. See you tonight at worship."

***

Steven pressed Brady about his promise. "So, when are you going to call your mom?"

"She doesn't want me. Why would she come all this way to watch me play something she's heard a zillion times already?" He led Steven into the chapel and looked for a place to sit. The front rows were filled, though there was still plenty of time before evening worship started.

"But you promised you'd call her if Zeke didn't send you home."

"Yeah, well, I didn't think I'd be here for the talent show." Brady pretended he didn't see Claire waving them toward the empty seats beside her.

"I've never known Zeke to send someone home," Steven said. "He's into more creative kinds of punishment."

"You could have told me that before you made me promise to call." He urged Steven in the opposite direction from Claire, but she'd already left her seat and was heading straight for them. No escape.

"Come on. I saved seats for you guys." She guided Steven through the maze of campers and led the way into the row. Brady breathed a little easier with Steven sitting between them, but Claire leaned over and tapped his arm. "Steven told

123

me what happened. Are you okay?"

Brady nodded. *As if she cares.* Still, he liked the idea that she was concerned about him.

"Taylor deserved it. Proud of ya!" She raised her hand for a high-five.

Brady slapped it and sat up straighter in the seat. Maybe now she'd see him as more than a fourth-grader. A hand on his shoulder made him look up.

"What's the good word?" Zeke raised one white eyebrow in an expectant look.

Brady closed his eyes, trying to remember that first word. "B-B-Bless those who curse you. Pray for those who mistreat you."

"Very good. Now, wait just a minute." Zeke stopped Taylor as he walked by, put an arm about his shoulder and brought him around to face Brady. He asked Taylor to recite his verse, then said, "This may seem childish to you boys, but I think it's important to ask forgiveness when we've wronged someone. Would either of you like to go first?"

Taylor's lips pressed tight together. He avoided looking at Brady, seemingly more interested in the conversation between Steven and Claire.

Claire shushed Steven. "Wait a minute. Shh."

Oddly, the prayer Matt had suggested Brady pray earlier popped into his mind. *God, bless Taylor any way you want.*

Brady opened his mouth. "I'm sorry I jumped you. It won't happen again." He meant it. How weird was that?

Taylor inhaled, opened his mouth as if to speak, then looked down at the floor. He crossed his arms over his chest, hands snug in his armpits. "Yeah, same here. Sorry." He raised his head and looked behind him, as if something exciting were happening on the other side of the room.

"Thank you, gentlemen." Zeke gave each boy's shoulder a squeeze. "And Steven, you're a witness. They both promised it won't happen again. If either one breaks his word, I trust you'll let me know."

"Deal!" Steven elbowed Brady as Zeke and Taylor walked away. "Hear that? Zeke doesn't like it when you break a promise."

***

Brady leaned sideways to see around the head of the kid in front of him. A familiar figure took shape on Zeke's drawing pad.

"How many of you talk with God?" Zeke faced the audience and held up his index finger. "I didn't say to Him, but with Him. There's a difference. Most of the time, we treat God like this guy."

"What guy?" Steven whispered.

"Santa Claus," Brady said. "He's drawing a picture of Santa."

Zeke shaded in the red suit while he spoke. "Once a year, we communicate our list of requests to Santa. When he fails to give us what we asked for, we get angry and decide he's not real." He looked to the audience for confirmation, peeking over the top of his reading glasses at them. "Is that what you do when your parents say no to something you want? Decide they're not real?"

Laughter rippled through the chapel.

"Of course not. But don't we do that very thing to God? Let's pretend for a minute that you treat your parents that way. How would they react if the only time you ever spoke to them is when you want something? Or if the only time your friends talk to you is to ask a favor, would your friendship last very long?"

Zeke's words made Brady think. Not too long ago, he and his mom talked a lot, about almost everything. Lately, though, he mostly just answered her questions about which friend he was hanging out with, what movie they were watching. Or he'd ask her to take him somewhere, or buy something he needed. Was that why she didn't want him anymore, because he acted like she was Santa Claus? When was the last time he'd told her what was going on at school or that he dreamed of being a professional trumpet player someday?

What had happened to make them stop talking to each other? Mom hadn't exactly been easy to talk to since she married Richard. Lately, she always looked tired. And she'd started chewing her lip again.

Maybe Steven was right about the talent show. If Brady could persuade her to come without Richard, maybe they could talk like they used to. Maybe she'd change her mind and let him come home.

Or maybe not. If she only wanted Richard and didn't care about him anymore, he might as well run away. He'd never seriously thought about doing that before. It kind of popped out while he was talking to Steven. *Would Mom miss me? Would she care enough to look for me?* He pulled his attention back to what Zeke was saying.

"Santa only comes around once a year, but God is a constant presence. He's with you no matter what time of the day it is or what time of year it is and no matter where you are. Santa's only reason for existence is to fulfill your wishes, like a genie in a bottle. That's not real." Zeke drew a thick, black circle around his picture, then added an X over Santa.

"We don't pray to Santa. We pray to our Creator God who is great enough to hang the stars in the sky and call each one by name. We pray to a God who is personal enough to know your name, so personal He knows the number of hairs on your head. He sees your life from beginning to end and knows what you need today, tomorrow, next week, next year. He promises to hear us when we call to Him. And when we cry for help, He answers, 'Here I am.' Let's talk with him right now."

Zeke bowed his head to pray.

An idea popped into Brady's head. It needed more thought, but he might keep his promise to Steven after all.

CHAPTER 13

Brady's eyes opened long before sunrise Thursday morning. His mind churned with indecision. If he decided to invite Mom to the talent show, it couldn't wait until tomorrow. He had to call her today.

At breakfast, he almost mentioned it to Steven, but clamped his mouth shut instead. Most of the time, Steven's cheerful confidence inspired him. But his friend didn't understand family conflicts, divorce, and stuff like that. Steven would only pester him to make the call, something he might regret later.

But what if Steven was right? If he didn't try to talk with Mom, he'd be living with Dad for sure. His pulse raced at the possibility of more rejection from Mom, but the alternative made it worth the risk.

On the way back to the cabin after Rec, Brady announced his decision. "I'm keeping my promise to you."

Steven stopped short, pulling back on Brady's elbow. A grin spread across his face. "Seriously?"

"Yeah. I've got it figured, what I'll say and how I'll say it. I think it'll work. But what phone do I use?"

"Zeke's office. Matt can take you. Come on, let's see if he's in his room." They hurried to the cabin where Steven rapped on Matt's door.

"Enter." Matt sat cross-legged on his bed, a book in his lap. "Hey, men. What's up?"

Steven blurted out, "Brady needs to call home right away."

Matt tipped his head to one side, eyeing Brady. "Are you sick?"

"No. I want to invite my mom to the talent show."

Matt shoved some clothes from the end of his bed and closed his book. "Sit down and tell me about it."

Steven leaned against the doorframe. Brady sat on the bed. "I've decided I'll apologize for talking back to her on Sunday, then tell her they want me to do the final act in the talent show on Friday."

"You think she'll come?"

"If not, I'll ask her to do it as a favor. Tomorrow's my birthday. It's the only birthday gift I really want."

Matt winced. "What if she still says no? Can you handle that?"

Brady shifted his position on the bed, wiped a drop of sweat crawling down the side of his face, and closed his eyes. Was he kidding himself? Had the shock from Sunday worn off? He wanted to believe she'd come, but what if she said no?

Matt bumped Brady's knee with his fist. "Don't get me wrong. I'm all for it if you think she'll come. I just don't want to see you get hurt again."

Brady inhaled and let his breath out slowly. With forced confidence, he said, "I'll be okay."

A grim expression settled onto Matt's face. He dropped his book on the floor and stood up. "All right. You have to call from Zeke's office. Let's go."

Brady's hands grew sweaty as they neared the main building. What if Mom wasn't home? What if she couldn't, or wouldn't, come? Maybe this wasn't the great idea he'd thought it was. It had kept him awake last night and gnawed at his mind all morning. Still, he had to try, like when he jumped off the diving board. If he didn't, he'd always be sorry he didn't take the chance.

Zeke was at his desk when Matt tapped on the open door. "Brady wants to call his mom and invite her to the talent show. Is this a good time for him to use the phone?"

"Come on in." Zeke closed a folder and dropped it into a side drawer. "Give me just a minute, Brady."

"Should I say my verse to you first?" Brady moved to stand in front of the desk.

A corner of Zeke's mouth lifted. "I'd like that."

"Bless those who curse you. Pray for those who mistreat you. Luke 6:28."

Zeke turned the phone around, lengthened the cord and set it in front of Brady. "Pull one of those chairs up to the desk here. That door locks automatically when it closes, but you can open it from the inside. Just be sure to close it when you leave." He came around the desk and took Steven's arm, guiding him out of the office. "Why don't we all wait out here?"

The door clicked shut. Brady stared at the phone as if it were a vicious dog threatening to bite. He picked up the receiver. The dial tone buzzed in his ear. He rehearsed the conversation in his mind while his finger punched ten numbers on the phone's keypad. It rang once, and three whistle tones sounded in his ear.

A woman's voice said, "We're sorry. Your call cannot be completed as dialed. You must dial a one or a zero first. Please hang up and try again."

He held the receiver out and stared at it, his brows scrunched together. A one or a zero? What for? He studied the keypad and carefully punched in his mom's cell number, beginning with a one.

His mouth went dry with the second ring. It was almost too much to hope that she was alone, that Richard wasn't home yet. He waited through four rings. Her voicemail usually picked up after five. If she didn't answer, should he leave a message or not?

Click. "Hello?"

"Mom! It's me." He gripped the receiver with both hands.

"Brady? What are you calling for? Are you sick?"

"No, I . . . I'm in the talent show. Tomorrow night. They want me to do the grand finale. Can you come and watch?" This wasn't at all how he'd planned it. He meant to apologize before telling her about the talent show.

"You want me to drive all the way up there again?"

"Yeah, but first, I'm sorry for what I said to you on Sunday. You're not at all like Dad. I didn't mean it." His mother said something, but her voice sounded muffled. Richard's voice in the background came through short and clipped. Why was he home so early?

Brady pressed on. "All the kids in the talent show get to invite their parents. You can stay overnight here at the camp, and we'll go home the next day." Did she catch the part about going home?

"I'm sorry, Brady."

"But Mom, did you hear what I said? I apologize."

"Yes, I heard that and I appreciate it. But I can't go up there tomorrow."

He clutched the receiver tight against his ear and tried to suck moisture back into his mouth. Richard's voice rose in the background, sounding angry.

Brady's chances were slipping away. "Mom, please? It's my birthday. Can't you come up and watch the show?" He hated the whiny tone in his voice.

"Honey, I can't."

"Pleease? Make it my birthday present. You don't have to get me anything else. Just come for the show. Richard doesn't have to come if he doesn't want to."

"I'm sorry, Brady. I'll send your birthday present to your dad's house."

"No! I don't want to live with Dad! Please, Mom."

Richard's voice was louder now, deep and threatening.

"I'm sorry, Brady. I can't talk now."

"Mom! Wait!"

"I have to go. G'bye."

"Mom!" The phone clicked. Brady's hand shook until he slammed the receiver down onto the base. His whole body trembled as he sank against the back of the chair. His chest was caving in and crushing his lungs, his breathing heavy and difficult.

It hadn't gone at all the way he'd planned. Maybe if Richard hadn't been there, his mom would've been more willing to talk with him.

He hated that man. Brady'd tried to like him, especially when Mom told him they were getting married. She'd seemed happy, at least for a little while. But there was something about

Richard he didn't trust. What did Mom see in the guy? More important, what did he sense that his mom apparently couldn't see?

A knock on the door interrupted his thoughts. Brady rose to open it. Steven stood on the other side.

"What did she say?"

Brady avoided looking at Matt and worked to keep his voice casual. "She's busy."

Steven's shoulders fell. "You're kidding!"

Brady shrugged. "She already had something planned."

"Are you okay?" Matt's voice suggested he wasn't fooled.

Brady dipped his head, stepped out of Zeke's office and closed the door behind him. "Yeah, I'm okay." He met Matt's gaze. "Really, I'm fine. I'll be all right."

Matt's eyes narrowed slightly. His jaw twitched, but he said nothing.

Steven reached out for Brady's arm. When he found it, he landed a light punch to his shoulder. "I'm really sorry, Brady."

"It's okay. I didn't expect her to come up anyway." Brady looked straight at Matt, challenging him to disagree.

Matt's nostrils flared as he exhaled. "All right, then. I'm going back to the cabin." He turned on his heel. The slap of his flip-flops echoed down the hall.

"So," Steven asked, "what do you want to do now? You wanna swim?"

Brady turned up his lip. "Not really." *I don't want to do anything, except maybe slam my fist into something.*

"I know. Let's take out a canoe and this time, you can steer."

"I don't know how." *And I don't want to know either.*

"Come on. I'll show you." Steven reached for Brady's arm.

134

"Are there any canoes left? I thought Claire said some other group needed them. That's why the carnival was held early."

"Zeke wouldn't let all of them go. There's bound to be a couple left."

Brady dragged his feet as they headed off to the boat dock, hoping the canoes would all be gone. But Steven was right. Two were held back for the campers, and one of them was returning to the dock as he and Steven descended the stairs. He took the life jackets Ryan offered, gave one to Steven then fastened the straps on his own. He gave them an extra tug before guiding Steven to the canoe.

The air had grown sticky, making his neck and chest already sweaty under the life vest. Clouds piled up too. Every so often, they blocked the sun for a bit, providing a minute or two of welcome shade. His mind kept replaying the phone conversation.

Steven climbed into the bow of the canoe and settled onto the seat. "You sit in back, so you can see what I'm doing with the paddle."

Brady took the rear seat, swaying backwards when Ryan pushed them off. The sensations were different back here, with the canoe out in front of him. The impression of gliding through the water thrilled him, and it wasn't as scary as it had been the first day they went out. Was that the result of practice? He'd survived being dumped out of the canoe. Maybe Steven's dad was right, after all. Once you experience the worst, you can deal with anything.

Steven began his instruction before they cleared the buoys for the swim area.

"If you're paddling on the right, and you want to turn to the right, reach the paddle out as far as you can before putting it in the water. Then as you pull it back, pull toward you. Like this." He drew his paddle through the water in a semi-circle.

Brady imitated, leaning a little too far out so that the canoe tipped. He almost landed in the water again. "Sorry."

"No problem. Try it again." Steven shifted his weight to counterbalance.

Brady's thoughts kept going back to the phone call as he reached out again, pulling the paddle toward him. The motion was awkward and stiff. There wasn't much change at first, but soon the canoe pointed toward the swimming area.

"Okay, I think I've got it." He dipped his paddle in again, pulling hard against the water's resistance. The canoe turned toward shore.

Steven hoisted his paddle in the air. "I feel it. We're turning. Okay, now, to turn the other way, put your paddle in closer to the canoe. But when you pull back, at the end of the stroke, push out away from you. Like this."

Brady mimicked Steven's actions. The canoe swayed back toward their original direction. His thoughts swayed back to his mother's voice. It sounded different, especially after he'd heard Richard's voice. Not worried, exactly. More like...scared. Yes, it was fear he'd heard in her voice. What was she afraid of? Or maybe he should ask who. Was it Richard?

Steven interrupted his thoughts. "Hey, you want to do circles?"

"Sure." Brady didn't care what they did, as long as he could think.

"Keep doing what you're doing." Steven reached his paddle out to the left and pulled it toward him in an arc.

The canoe swung in a complete circle once, twice. Brady's attention was elsewhere. He needed to be at home, to find out what was going on and why his mom was scared.

"Had enough?" Steven pulled in his paddle and twisted halfway around in his seat.

"Yeah."

"Are you okay? You're not saying much."

Brady needed more time to think. He had to keep Steven occupied. "Yeah, I'm good. Let's keep paddling. I want to practice a little more. Then we can head back."

"Okay, you're in charge." Steven faced forward again and dipped his paddle in the water.

How could he get home? Brady's mind searched for a solution. He couldn't wait for Saturday, in case Dad actually showed up to take him home. He needed to leave tonight. But how?

He dug his paddle into the water, pushing the canoe farther out on the lake. He wouldn't get very far on foot. Besides, walking home would take longer than waiting for his dad. He and Mom had driven through a nearby town on the way up here. Maybe there was a bus station there. He still had most of the money Mom gave him, but how much would a bus ticket cost?

Run away? The very idea brought a suffocating tightness to Brady's chest, and his sweaty hands slid on the smooth neck of the paddle. Still, the memory of his mother's voice stirred his determination to get home. He'd wait until dark to make it easier to hide, in case Zeke or anyone came looking for him. They'd look on the highway that ran past the camp's entrance first. But what other way was there?

"Whereabouts are we?" Steven turned halfway around.

Brady noted their position past the boundary line. "Farther than we should be. I'll turn us around and head back to shore." He extended the paddle as far as he could reach, drove it into the water and pulled it toward him. A couple more strokes and they were facing Rustic Knoll's shoreline. Surprising how far they'd come in only a few minutes.

That's it! Brady sat up straight, looked toward the shore then looked behind him. They were maybe a third of the way across the lake. It would probably take longer without Steven to help paddle, but no one would expect him to escape across the lake. It was perfect. Even if they discovered his route, they'd search that shoreline for hours while he hitched a ride into town and caught a bus for home. All he needed to do was pick up a paddle and life jacket that weren't locked up.

Brady smiled and thrust his paddle through the water with renewed energy. He was going home.

CHAPTER 14

Brady scooted his dinner tray along the counter behind Claire. Steven followed, but Brady wasn't worried about him seeing the food he stuffed into his pockets. It could be a long time before he ate again. As soon as Claire pushed ahead, he swiped a couple packages of soup crackers.

Janie pushed through the door to the kitchen and eyed the food left on the buffet. Her face lit up when she saw them. "How are my favorite campers tonight?"

Steven leaned toward her. "Janie, I'm hungry for cake. Could you make some for tomorrow?"

Her dark eyebrows arched up. "What kind of cake?"

"Birthday cake." Steven grinned and jerked his thumb in Brady's direction.

Brady froze. He never imagined Steven would tell.

Janie clapped her hands. "Is tomorrow your birthday?"

Claire gripped his forearm. "Seriously? You didn't tell

us."

"He told me." Steven pushed his chest out. Claire put her hands on her hips and stuck her tongue out at him, as if he could see it.

"A birthday cake it is. What kind do you like? Vanilla? Chocolate? Spice? Lemon?" Janie ticked off the flavors on her fingers.

Brady shrugged away the attention. "I like any kind." On second thought, it was kind of nice having someone make a big deal about it, especially since Mom wasn't around.

"Oh, come on," Claire said. "Janie can make anything. What's your favorite?" Her eyes sparkled, and he couldn't help smiling at her excitement.

Steven nudged him. "Go ahead. It's your birthday." "Fifteen?" Claire asked.

"Fourteen." He hated to admit he was younger.

She leaned back. "Really? You seem older."

He clamped his lips together to keep a smile from breaking out.

"Pick a flavor," Janie prompted. "What's your favorite?"

"Carrot." It slipped out before he could stop it.

"Carrot cake?" Steven's lip curled up and his nose wrinkled. "What kind of birthday cake is that?"

"You've never tasted my mom's. All that cream cheese frosting." He licked his lips.

Janie slapped the buffet counter. "You got it. Carrot cake with lots of cream cheese frosting."

Brady moved on to fill his glass with soda, marveling at Janie's kindness. Too bad he wouldn't be here to enjoy it.

***

"Time for evening worship." Matt hustled the stragglers from the cabin. "Everybody out. Let's go."

Brady slipped the crackers he'd taken into his backpack and zipped it shut. Even with everything he might need for the trip, it wasn't very full. Maybe it would attract less attention that way. He set the backpack on the floor by Steven's bed, camouflaging his trumpet, which he'd conveniently neglected to return to Matt's room. The instrument weighed more than his backpack. But if he left it here, he might never get it back.

Claire was waiting for them at the chapel door. "It's about time. Come on. Probably no seats left up front."

She led them up the center aisle, her head swiveling left, right, left, checking each row for three seats together. When she found them, she squeezed past the kids sitting near the aisle. Brady and Steven followed her.

Not the easy escape he'd hoped for. Brady gazed out the windows. Though the sun had set, there was still enough light to cast blue shadows from the cross-shaped window onto the stage. A few kids hurried up and down the aisle, looking for a place to sit. He waited until the music started, then leaned over and spoke into Steven's ear.

"Need to hit the bathroom. If Zeke starts before I get back, I'll sit by the door. Don't worry about me." Steven nodded, and Brady squeezed through the row until he reached the aisle. He hurried to the back and scurried out the door.

Ryan stopped him. "Where're you going?"

"Bathroom. Have to hurry so I don't miss Zeke." He kept going, hoping Ryan didn't see through his lie. He dashed toward the cabins, but circled behind and headed for the clinic, staying far enough from the chapel to keep from being seen through the windows. Hopefully, Willie hadn't gone fishing yet. That could ruin everything.

He tiptoed to the door and peeked through the window. Light from the clinic shone on the entryway floor. Nurse

Willie must be in there. Could he get in and open the closet door without getting caught?

Brady backed against the wall. His pulse pounded in his ears, and he fought to still his breathing. He was already in trouble with Zeke. He squeezed his eyes shut against the embarrassment and punishment if Nurse Willie caught him. Could he go through with this?

He had to. Compared to what he heard in his mom's voice, it was silly to worry about being caught. He peeked through the window again and laid his sweaty hand on the doorknob. Mouth open, tongue pressed against his teeth in concentration, he turned the knob. It didn't make a sound, even when he pulled the door open. He stepped inside and let it close until the latch rested gently against the jamb.

Now for the closet. Brady held his breath and turned the knob. The door swung open, revealing a mop, bucket, and other cleaning supplies, as well as the paddle and life jacket. In the clinic, Nurse Willie's footsteps shuffled back and forth. Was she talking to herself?

A thump on the floor startled him. The outer door clicked shut. Too scared to move or even breathe, Brady glanced at the clinic door. His heart pounded in his throat.

Nurse Willie stepped out and peered at him over her reading glasses. She held a fishing pole in her hand and thumped the handle on the floor. "I thought I heard someone come in. What's the matter, Brady? Poison ivy bothering you?"

He nodded, the words stuck in his throat.

"Well, come on, then. Let's get you fixed up. Aren't you supposed to be in worship?" She glanced at the closet. "Did I leave that door open? Close it for me, will you please?" She shook her head, setting the lures on her hat to tinkling. "One of these days, I'm going to forget to wake up in the morning." She turned back into the clinic.

Brady followed her, but left the door open. First Janie, and now Nurse Willie. He hated fooling people who were nice to him.

Willie shook the anti-itch spray and examined his ankles before blasting them with cool moisture. "That should do it. Looks like they're healing all right. Is Steven coming by for some antihistamine tonight?"

"Um, probably. I think so." He averted his eyes.

"All right then. Hurry back to chapel now." She put the spray back in the cupboard and took up her fishing rod again.

He nearly stumbled in his rush to leave, but slowed in the entryway. Reaching into the closet, he called a thank you while he pulled out the life jacket and paddle, counting on his voice to mask any noise. At Willie's "You're welcome," he closed the door. A second later, he sprinted up the path toward the cabin.

The last rays of sunlight grew dim. Brady set the gear down alongside the outer wall of the cabin. Guilt gnawed at him for stealing from Nurse Willie, but what else could he do? He moved around to peek through the screen door. A light burned in the bunkroom, but he heard no sounds.

"Anybody here?" He kept his voice low. No one answered. He opened the screen door, stopping when it started to screech, then squeezed through and snatched his backpack and trumpet from the bunkroom. Back outside, he shrugged the backpack onto his shoulders and slung the life jacket over one arm. Then, paddle in one hand and trumpet in the other, he stole along the edge of the woods.

In the deepening darkness, he tripped over a vine snaking across the ground, but managed to stay upright all the way to the lake. A bullfrog croaked and splashed into the water as he approached. He wrinkled his nose at the pungent, marshy smell, and used the paddle to scrape a mosquito off his arm. Another mosquito landed on his face, and soon, the air swarmed with the bloodthirsty insects. He batted them with the paddle, swung his trumpet case in an attempt to clear a path through them, but finally moved back from the edge of the water. Ugh. His shoes were soaked through and now his feet squished with every step.

Away from the marshy area, the ground rose from the lake, and Brady hurried along the edge near the campfire site. Tomorrow night, after the talent show, everyone would gather for a final campfire. Everyone, but him. He would have liked to say good-bye to Steven and Claire. Maybe after he got home, he'd look them up online.

The trumpet weighed heavy on his arm as he hurried past the swimming area and felt his way down the steps to the boat dock. In the dark, he squinted to find the two canoes where they lay overturned on the sand. No moonlight glistened on the lake, no stars winked at him from the sky. Odd how quickly clouds could move in. The nearest light came from a neighboring boathouse where figures moved around on the deck above it. Their voices carried on the breeze. Farther out, running lights marked the progress of motorboats crossing the lake.

Brady dropped his load to the sand and fit his fingers under the gunwale of the closest canoe. He lifted, but it was heavier than he expected. He moved to the canoe's midsection and lifted again, grunting as it came to rest on his shoulder while his hands searched for a better hold. He pushed, and the canoe tipped up on its side, teetered then fell away from him, scraping his shin as it came to rest on its hull.

"Ow!" He grabbed his leg and hopped on the other foot, rubbing his shin. A swift kick to the aluminum hull only made it worse. "Ouch!" Now, both his shin and his toe ached. He picked up his backpack and threw it into the canoe, then set his trumpet case next to it. With the life jacket strapped securely around his chest, he slipped the paddle into the stern and gave three strong shoves before the canoe slid into the water. He followed, jumping into the back. Water squished from his saturated shoes as he settled on the stern seat and pushed his paddle against the lake's sandy bottom.

Faint whoops and laughter told him evening worship was over. He'd have to hurry. He dug the paddle into the water and pulled back hard, eager to get away before anyone noticed. The canoe cleared the swimming buoys and headed into the cave-like darkness. Floodlights and decorative party lanterns marked residences on either side of the bay. Their light didn't reach the middle, but they helped him gauge his progress. He found a rhythm to the drops that fell from his paddle as the canoe whispered through the water. The wind increased, raising waves that pushed against the bow.

His eyes adjusted to the darkness, but once he left the bay, black night closed in around him. The lights from shore stretched away on either side, and it was difficult to gauge distance. Peering ahead, he targeted a spot between distant deck lights where he'd land and continue his journey on foot. A brief lighting of the sky exposed a silhouette of the trees on the far shore. A cool rush of wind followed, and moments later, a gentle rumble vibrated through the air.

A storm? Now? He paused in mid-stroke. He was heading right into it. Maybe he should turn and head for the shore to his right. Was it the same distance? He couldn't be certain in the darkness.

Another noise made him twist in his seat, searching for the source. Starting soft and low like some kind of vibration, it soon grew louder, becoming more of a buzz. Distant running lights glowed high above the water, indicating a much bigger boat. They weren't wasting any time crossing the lake, and they were coming his way.

It couldn't be anyone from Rustic Knoll. Steven would try to find him, but they couldn't have figured out his escape yet. The lights advanced toward him, and then his gaze swept the length of his canoe. With no running lights, they'd never see him.

Forget the storm; he needed to get out of their way now.

He dug his paddle down, back, up and forward. Again. Switch sides. Repeat. Faster. The boat bore down on him, probably about as far as the distance from his cabin to the beach. Was it the darkness that made it seem like the boat was following him?

"Hey! Watch out!"

Silly. They'd never hear him over the noise of the motor. But a light might get their attention. He dropped the paddle and grabbed the backpack at his feet. He unzipped the front pocket and felt around for his flashlight. Where was it? In a panic, he thrust his hand into the main cavity where his fingers closed around it. He drew it out and flicked the switch. Under other circumstances, he might have laughed at the puny beam that barely reached to the other end of his canoe. Still, maybe someone on the approaching boat would notice it. He kicked the pack away and waved the light at the motorboat. The monster kept coming.

Maybe if I turn parallel…

He held the flashlight beam up, his hand atop the paddle, and worked to swing the canoe around. At the last moment, he jumped to his feet and shone his flashlight at the boat's windshield. He screamed, but couldn't hear himself above the roar as the huge bow scraped against the canoe, shoving it aside like a toy. Brady gulped air just before his body slammed into the water.

Blackness everywhere. No daylight told him up from down. And the roar, now muffled by the water, moved away as quickly as it had come.

CHAPTER 15

Darkness. Everywhere.

Brady kicked, pumped his arms up, down. Which way was the surface? Something exerted a gentle but constant pressure against the back of his neck, and in seconds, his head broke the surface of the water. His life jacket! He'd done something right this time.

He blew water from his nose, coughed up what was left in his throat. Water plugged both ears, and he tilted his head, shook it, ducked beneath the surface to equalize the pressure and hopefully drain it. Where was the canoe? He peered through the darkness.

Lightning exposed the tree line again and reflected briefly off the aluminum craft. Brady dog-paddled over to the canoe and clung to the side. Could he climb back in? He gripped the gunwale and tried to lift his leg out of the water, up over the side. His weight on the gunwale made it dip below the water's surface, and water gushed into the canoe. He shifted from the center to the stern, near his seat, and tried again. He couldn't lift his leg high enough without tipping the canoe over. His backpack was probably soaked through by now. And his trumpet. Water would seep through the cracks where the case opened and soak the lining. The brassy gold finish would tarnish quickly. How much additional damage would a soaking cause?

More lightning lit up a mountainous cloudbank. Moments later, thunder rumbled low and distant. He had to get out of here before that storm hit. Another attempt to climb into the canoe only allowed more water to flood the inside. With an angry growl, he pounded his fist against the aluminum hull. Which would be worse when the storm hit, being in the water or in an aluminum canoe? Not much difference, as far as he could tell.

Even if he made it into the canoe, he had no paddle. It was in his hand when he fell. Must be floating out there on the water somewhere, but he couldn't see it. Not without his flashlight, which had probably sunk to the bottom of the lake.

Another burst of lightning. Brady studied the shore on every side of him. Camp looked farther away than the other three sides, though darkness made it difficult to know for sure. The lights to his right looked closest. He'd have to swim for it, and fast. Lightning flashed every few minutes now. He clung to the canoe, gathering his strength. What about the trumpet? Would the canoe capsize in the storm? He hated the thought of his horn settling to the bottom, next to his useless flashlight.

He couldn't think about that now. Lightning splashed across a chunk of sky and thunder grumbled. He pushed off from the canoe and started swimming. One of his shoes had come off. Now he kicked off the other one as well, letting it drift to the bottom. Just like Hansel and Gretel, leaving a trail of crumbs only a diver could find. At least it made it more difficult for anyone to track him.

Brady itched to take off the life jacket too. It was uncomfortable and made swimming difficult, but he didn't dare let it go. His arms soon tired, and he turned onto his back and continued kicking. He closed his eyes so they wouldn't have to readjust to the darkness after every lightning flash. How fast was the storm moving? There was nothing he could use to judge its progress, no way to tell time. Had he been swimming for five minutes? Or twenty? No idea. He turned back onto his stomach. The shore didn't look any closer. Maybe he was swimming in circles, like people lost in the woods.

Treading water, Brady studied the shore for something to aim at. One floodlight shone brighter than the rest. Darkness engulfed most of its surroundings, except for a small dock and the side of the old boathouse where it was mounted. He took a deep breath, then poked his head into the water and swam as hard as he could. The life jacket kept him near the surface, but it also restricted how high he could lift his head when he came up for breath. A wave splashed in his face as he inhaled. He choked and nearly coughed his guts out.

"Augh!" Though loud in his ears, the darkness and wind swallowed his shout. Why did everything have to be so hard? He just wanted to get home to Mom. Was there something wrong with that? He looked up into the starless sky.

"God! Are you there? If you can see me, do something! Help me!"

Nothing. No answer.

He had to keep going, had to reach Mom. His muscles protested, but he pushed on, remembering to breathe on his right, away from the wind-driven waves.

One. Two. Three. He counted twenty breaths and looked up to measure his progress. The counting gave his mind something to do besides thinking about the thunder's increasing volume. Still, the shore didn't look any closer even after several intervals. He chafed against the life jacket's restrictions. What if he wrapped it around his waist instead? That would keep him afloat but wouldn't interfere with his strokes. Nineteen. Twenty.

The light at the boathouse still looked impossibly far away, and he was off course. Probably pushed aside by the waves. He untied the top lashes of his jacket and unbuckled the bottom strap. Careful to not let go, he opened the vest and pushed it down around his waist, kicking furiously to keep his head above water. He wrapped the long bottom strap around his body and the jacket itself twice, sliding the buckle out as far as it would go. Now, the jacket snuggled against him and he could move his arms a lot easier.

He started out again, his arms pulling hard to rest his legs. One, two, three. At twenty, he raised his head, but the shore still didn't look any closer than when he started out. Was his mind playing tricks on him? Maybe it was too far. He'd never reach it. The storm would hit and he'd be struck by lightning, right here in the water. Whatever made him think he should run for home, anyway? What good would he be against a man like Richard?

His arms ached. Cramps curled his feet and his lungs burned for a normal breath. The chill wind across his wet body made him shiver. At this rate, he'd never reach shore. No one would care anyway. Claire thought he was childish. Steven might care, but not Mom or Dad, the people who mattered.

Brady turned over to float on his back. Was this how

Jonah felt just before the fish swallowed him? Hopeless? Ready to give up? He imagined what it would be like to drown—his lungs filling with water, struggling to breathe. How soon would he lose consciousness?

Lightning snaked across the sky, and thunder boomed loud enough to startle him. His hand moved to the buckle on his life jacket. He just needed to unsnap it and his pain could be over. Forever.

"Brady? Brady!" The voice was faint, distant.

Who was it? Where was it coming from? He raised his head and twisted around in the water. Someone must be looking for him, but who?

"Brady!" It sounded like Matt. But where was he? There were no boats on the water, at least none with running lights.

"Brady!"

"Here! I'm here!" Brady shouted as loud as he could, but it sounded like a whisper in the roar of wind and crashing thunder. He listened again. The voice seemed to come from the shore, possibly even the boathouse with the bright light.

"I'm coming! Wait for me." Brady nearly cried with relief. His arms churned despite the pain. He ignored the fatigue in his legs and kicked, stopping only when he needed to gulp some air. A moment later, he started in again.

The next time he looked, he'd made a little progress, but he didn't hear Matt calling anymore.

"Matt? You still there?" He turned circles in the water, listening. "Where are you?" His heart dropped like a rock to the lake bottom until he heard his name again.

"Brady! Braa-a-ady!"

He waved an arm in the air. "Here! I'm here. I'm coming!" He started swimming again, uncertain if the drops on his back were raindrops or simply water splashed up from his swimming. It didn't matter. He had to get to shore, had to let Matt know he was there.

Lightning lit the sky overhead. A moment later, thunder clapped, but he pressed on. His lungs burned like they'd explode any minute now. His arms grew numb. They rose out of the water and flopped forward. He alternated strokes, using the crawl as much as possible but switching to the breaststroke when he could no longer lift his arms or when his feet cramped. Occasionally, he'd flip onto his back to give his breathing a chance to recover. But always, he moved forward. The light on that boathouse grew bigger, brighter.

"Matt! You still there?" He needed the reassurance, the encouragement.

"Brady?"

Close enough now to make out shapes along the shore, he looked for a lone figure. Matt must be standing in a shadow. Maybe he took shelter under an eave from the raindrops falling big and heavy. They pelted Brady as bolts of lightning split the night sky. The thunder's vibration shook him.

"Hang on! I'm almost there." He willed his limbs to pull, kick, move. Being in the water grew more dangerous every second. He needed to get onto dry land before a lightning bolt fried him. The dock was close, but he still couldn't touch bottom here. The lifejacket dragged on him, even while keeping him afloat. As tired as he was, it was tempting to unbuckle it and let it go. But no, he wouldn't risk drowning this close to his goal.

The floodlight on the side of the boathouse beckoned him while casting ghostly light on nearby trees. Their branches whipped in wild frenzy in the wind. Raindrops peppered his back like BB's. He still couldn't see Matt anywhere, even in the brief moments when lightning brightened the world like midday. Still, the intermittent calling of his name spurred him on until he neared the dock.

Twenty yards away, he was forced to stop and catch his breath. His stomach lurched from the amount of water he'd swallowed, but the nausea disappeared as soon as his toes tapped sand. If he'd had any strength left, he'd have let out a happy whoop. Good thing the water supported him, because his legs buckled when he tried to stand. His cold fingers fumbled with the buckle on the life jacket until it finally let go. He pulled the vest up around his neck again and half walked, half floated to the dock. Breathless, he called for Matt.

"I'm here. I made it."

His fingers closed around the rungs of the ladder on the dock as thunder crashed above him. He dragged his body onto the dock and lay still, letting the rain hammer his back, neck and limbs. Where was Matt? Why didn't he come help him? Brady rolled onto his side and called.

"Matt? I made it. Where are you?"

No answer.

His teeth chattered as rain stung his face and arms. His t-shirt and shorts offered little protection from the rain's lashing. The seconds between lightning and thunder told him the storm was directly overhead. He needed to find shelter, get off this metal dock. Flinging off his sodden life jacket, he pushed himself up and gingerly tried to stand. His legs held him only a moment before they collapsed. Even his arms rebelled at the pressure of crawling on hands and knees to the boathouse. He reached up and tried the doorknob, but it refused to turn.

"Nooo!" He shook the door, pounded his fist against the weathered wood. Tears slid down his cheeks, mingling with rain, and he fell against the old door, shoulder butting the splintery wood. The door gave way and he tumbled inside.

Sheltered from the wind and rain, Brady curled his body up and tried to draw warmth into his arms and legs. The chilly concrete floor did nothing to still his constant shivering. The flood light outside illuminated only a small area inside the door, but nearby water slapped against something solid. A dull thumping or rubbing sound too, and the air held an odd mix of scents: lake, fish, gasoline, motor oil.

Lightning momentarily brightened the scene through two windows on the hanging garage door. A pontoon boat bobbed about on restless water, straining against tie-ropes and shifting back and forth between rubber bumpers.

Thunder pounded the roof. Beneath him, the concrete vibrated. The building shuddered and creaked in the wind, trembling with each roll of thunder. Tree branches clawed at the roof. He shoved the door closed and huddled, shivering and wet, palms pressed against his ears.

Clenching his teeth, Brady swallowed hard. He'd never been so scared. Scared. Tired. Cold. And utterly alone. Dad didn't care. Mom didn't want him. Matt left him. Even nature, it seemed, was against him. And where was God? Nowhere that he could see.

Lightning blazed through the rain-spattered windows, temporarily blinding him with its brilliance. But in that moment of light, he glimpsed something on the pontoon boat. He closed his eyes tight until the image inside his eyelids faded. Feeling his way, he crept along the floor until he touched the side of the boat and grabbed a towel hanging over the side railing. One end was damp from the water splashing up, but he threw it around his shoulders, hugging it tight around his back and clutching it to his chest.

Another burst of light revealed a second towel hanging on the opposite side. He gripped the side rail with both hands, using the motion of the boat lifting on a surge to pull himself up. Steadying himself, he waited as the boat fell and rose again. At the next low, he flung his leg over the railing and his body followed as the swell lifted him up and over. He dropped onto the floor of the boat and rolled to the other side where he pulled the second towel around him. Warmth seeped back through his skin, into his blood, and hopefully all the way to his bones.

The rocking of the boat grew less violent as the storm passed. He found it soothing, even relaxing, except for the hard floor. He sat up and groped his way to the bench seat at the back, easing onto the cushion. His muscles ached as much from shivering as from exertion. He wrapped one towel around his legs and kept one around his upper body as he stretched out on the cushion, willing his body to stop trembling.

So tired. So...very...tired.

CHAPTER 16

Muted voices intruded on his consciousness, but he wasn't ready to open his eyes.

"Heard the report over the police scanner last night. Came down here this morning to check for storm damage and found him snuggled up like that. Figured he's probably the one you're looking for."

The voices were unfamiliar and he turned away, waiting for the gentle rocking to lull him back to dreamland.

"That's him. Thank you, Lord! In all my years as camp director, I've never had to call a parent and tell them we couldn't find their child—until last night. I hope it never happens again."

That voice was familiar, but he couldn't quite place it. Was it a teacher from school? A jolt interrupted the pleasant rocking, and someone shook his shoulder.

"Brady? Time to wake up, son."

Brady opened his eyes and looked around. This wasn't like any bedroom he'd ever seen before. Where was he? He turned his head.

Zeke peered at him. The older man knelt on one knee beside Brady and helped him sit up. "Praise God, you're safe. Are you hurt?"

Brady dropped the towel from his shoulders and stretched. His arms and legs were stiff and tight. "No, just sore." He rubbed the sleep from his eyes and pulled at his wrinkled shorts and t-shirt. Memories of last night came and went like waves washing up on shore.

Zeke's expression showed concern, but no hint of the scolding Brady expected. "Are you hungry?"

Starving, now that he thought about it. He nodded.

"Good. Janie's waiting to feed you pancakes, French toast, eggs, anything you want. Let's go back to camp." He helped Brady to his feet and held on while he took his first stiff steps. "Can you walk all right?"

"I'll make it." His muscles loosened up as he stepped off the pontoon boat.

A police officer in a brown uniform waited near the boathouse door, thumbs hooked in his belt. Another man wearing a faded Hawaiian shirt, shorts and deck shoes reached out and ruffled Brady's hair when he walked by.

"Next time, come on up and knock on my door. No need to spend the night out here, 'specially in a storm like that." He smiled and patted him on the back, then pulled the door open. The man pressed in the lock on the doorknob, jiggled it and looked at the officer.

"Can't figure out how he got in. I put this new knob on a few weeks ago." He scratched his head.

The officer rapped his knuckle against the door where the

wood was starting to splinter. "Should've replaced the whole door."

Zeke motioned toward a stone stairway. The rustic steps climbed a hillside to a two-story house with tall windows overlooking the lake. Brady flinched at lifting his knee high enough to set his foot on the first step. About halfway up the hill, his sore legs demanded rest.

"Are you sure you're okay?" Zeke sat beside him while the other two men continued to the top. "We found your canoe with your backpack and trumpet. It washed ashore near camp."

"You've got my trumpet?" Brady shook his head in amazement. He'd tried not to imagine it lying on the bottom of the lake. The case was probably ruined after being out in the storm all night. How well had the trumpet itself survived? He'd have to dry it off, pull out the valves and inspect it. Energized, he jumped to his feet. "Let's go get it."

Zeke chuckled and followed him. A sheriff's squad car waited at the top. The officer opened the back door for them to climb in.

Brady hesitated. "Am I under arrest?"

"No." Zeke grinned. "A little trouble, maybe, but you're not under arrest. We're just thankful you were found alive and relatively well. Let's get you back to camp."

Brady climbed in and buckled his seat belt. "Why the police car, if I'm not under arrest?"

"When we couldn't find you last night, I notified the sheriff's department. They've been out looking for you. Mr. Breidenbach is on the volunteer fire department and heard about you on his police scanner last night. When he found you in his boat this morning, he called it in. Officer Scott picked me up on the way so I could identify you."

Brady stared at his bare feet and wiggled his toes. The

shoes he'd pestered Mom to buy were at the bottom of the lake. What would she say about all this? Was she okay? Yesterday seemed like ages ago.

"Does my mom know I ran away?"

Zeke nodded. "I called her right after I called the police."

"What did she say?"

"Not much. I think I woke her up. Would you like to let her know you're all right?" Zeke pulled out his cell phone and handed it to him.

Brady hesitated, not sure what to expect after his last phone call. At last, he took the phone and dialed her cell number. It rang several times before a recorded voice told him his call was important to her and asked him to leave a message.

What should he say? "Hey, Mom, it's me." Duh! "I'm okay, in case you're wondering." He paused again before saying good-bye and cutting off the call.

Zeke took the phone back and shifted his position in the seat. He faced Brady, his arm resting along the top of the back seat. "Tell me about your adventure."

Brady glanced at Officer Scott and hung his head. "I wanted to go home so I . . .I took Nurse Willie's paddle and life preserver out of her closet."

"And you made it all the way to Mr. Breidenbach's before the storm?"

Brady avoided Officer Scott's frequent glances in the rear-view mirror as he described the accident with the larger boat, his swim to shore and how tempted he was to just give up and die.

Zeke's eyebrows arched at the mention of Matt calling. "What made you think it was Matt?"

Brady shrugged. "It was his voice. Why?"

Zeke rubbed his mustache with his thumb. "And you swam from the middle of the lake? In the storm?" He appeared to consider that for a minute, then asked, "Did this have anything to do with the trouble between you and Taylor?"

Brady shot him a startled look. "No. I just needed to get home, that's all." He hadn't given Taylor a single thought since the phone call to Mom.

The squad car pulled into the Rustic Knoll parking lot and Zeke instructed the officer to drop them off at the clinic.

"What about breakfast?" Brady's stomach growled, loud enough for all to hear.

"I'll have Janie send someone down with a tray for you. I want Nurse Willie to check you over before we do anything else."

The car rolled to a stop in front of the clinic. Officer Scott got out and opened the door for them, stopping Brady when he climbed out.

"A lot of stuff happens to kids who run away, and none of it is good. Next time, talk to Zeke here instead. He's a good man." He winked and gave Brady's shoulder a light squeeze, then turned to go. Zeke called his thanks as he ushered Brady into the clinic.

Willie closed a cabinet door and faced him with hands planted firmly on her hips. Brady fidgeted under her scrutiny, grateful for Zeke's hands on his shoulders.

"He had a rough night in the lake, Willie. Check him over and make sure he's okay. I'll ask Janie to send down a breakfast tray."

Zeke left, and Nurse Willie directed him to sit on the bed and approached him with a stethoscope around her neck. He found it difficult to look her in the eye. Surely, by now she knew her gear was gone, and he was the thief. She stuck a thermometer in his mouth and waited for the electronic beep.

"He said *in* the lake. Didn't he mean *on* it?"

Brady opened his mouth to release the thermometer. "No, the rough part was in the water." His ears grew hot and his face burned. "I'm sorry I stole your paddle and life jacket."

Willie fixed him with a stern look that softened a bit. "I accept your apology. And I forgive you."

She said nothing more while she listened to his heart and breathing. He squirmed as the silence lengthened.

"Stick out your tongue and say 'ah'." She held his tongue down with a wooden tongue depressor. "Most kids wish they could stay here all summer. Can't say I've ever known anyone to run away from camp. Where were you going?"

"Home."

She tipped her head. Her dark eyes studied him. "You don't strike me as the homesick type."

He shrugged and looked at the floor. "I just wanted to go home."

Willie checked his eyes and ears, and asked a few questions about his ordeal before the door burst open and more than one pair of footsteps pounded through the entryway.

"Brady!" Claire left Steven in the doorway and raced to his side. She threw her arms around his shoulders and gave him a quick hug. "You're back. I was so worried about you. Are you all right?"

Better than ever. He couldn't keep the smile from his lips, even when Taylor appeared and leaned against the doorway. He gave Brady a brief nod before his gaze settled on Claire. Chris popped in as well, crowding the tiny clinic. Nurse Willie pulled a chair up next to the bed and guided Steven to it. Steven held his hand out and clasped Brady's, holding it in a tight fist.

"You lied. Said you were going to the head."

The anger in Steven's voice made Brady's stomach clinch as if punched. He'd not only stolen equipment, he'd lied to his friend.

"I was afraid you'd try to talk me out of leaving."

"Why'd you leave?" Steven loosened his grip.

He owed Steven an explanation, but not in front of all the others. He caught Willie's eye, hoping she'd rescue him.

"Don't you all need to be getting on to morning worship? You can talk to Brady later, after he's had a chance to eat some breakfast and get his strength back." She waved her hands to shoo everyone out of the clinic.

Taylor straightened. "Hey, I promise not to tease you about running anymore." His lips pulled into a friendly smirk, but his eyes sought Claire.

"Is that all you can say after what he's been through?" Claire rolled her eyes and shook her head. "Grow up, Taylor."

She gave Brady another hug before getting up to leave. Taylor's smirk wilted into a frown, and his shoulders drooped as he turned away.

Taylor? And Claire? Now the conversation made sense, the one he'd overheard between the two girls from his small group. They were talking about Taylor, not him. Was Taylor jealous of his friendship with Claire?

Steven released his hand and rose with a promise to return later. Claire guided Steven out the door behind Chris and Taylor. As Brady settled back on the bed, Willie encouraged him to lie down and rest. Last night was catching up with him again and he rolled over to get more comfortable when Matt arrived with a breakfast tray. His stomach rumbled at the scent of bacon. The butter-drenched toast beside a mound of scrambled eggs made his mouth water almost to the point of drooling.

Matt placed the tray on the bed beside him then stood back with hands on hips, looking him over. "I don't know whether to hug you or strangle you."

Nurse Willie cleared her throat. "No strangling in my clinic." She busied herself straightening up the cupboards and wiping down the counters.

Brady sat up and went to work devouring the eggs and bacon while sorting out his thoughts. If Matt hadn't been out in the storm, calling his name, he wouldn't be enjoying this breakfast right now. But Matt had left him, just like everyone else in his life.

Matt flipped around the chair left from Steven and straddled it, his arms across the back. "I wanted to come with the other kids, but Janie made me wait so I could bring the tray down. We all cheered when Zeke said they found you. I just wish you'd have come and talked to me—"

"You left me." Brady set the glass of orange juice on the tray and fixed his gaze on Matt.

The counselor's mouth fell open. His brows came together and his eyes moved quickly from side to side. "When? Yesterday, after you called your mom? From that look you gave me, I didn't think you wanted to talk in front of Steven."

"No, I mean last night." Brady swallowed a bite of toast. "You left me alone last night."

Matt held out his hands, palms up, and shook his head. "What are you talking about? You're the one who left last night."

Irritation burned in Brady's chest. "Yeah, and you came out to look for me, but you left me there."

Matt looked to Nurse Willie. She raised an eyebrow, hunched one shoulder, and went back to laying out fish hooks, corks, feathers and other tiny items on her desk. He turned back to Brady. "I wanted to go out and look for you. I begged Zeke to let me take the boat out, but he wouldn't let anyone leave. I was in the chapel all night."

Brady studied Matt through narrowed eyes. He didn't seem like the kind of guy who would lie, even to save himself embarrassment. But Brady was positive about what he'd heard. "You're lying."

"No, I'm not! Ask Steven. Ask Claire, and Chris. We were in the chapel all night. Even Taylor was there for a little while."

"Taylor? In the chapel? What for?"

"A prayer vigil. We spent all night praying for you." Matt jumped up and circled the tiny room, arms folded across his chest. He stopped and eyed Brady. "What do you mean, I left you?"

Brady pushed his breakfast tray away. How could Matt have called to him if he was in the chapel all night? "I heard you calling my name. A big motorboat knocked me out of the canoe. It was too far to swim to shore and the storm came up fast. I almost gave up, but I heard you calling." He searched for some sign of recognition in Matt's face, but found none. "You called my name. Every time I wanted to give up..." Had he really wanted to die out there? "I heard you calling. It saved me, knowing you were out there looking for me. That's the only reason I made it to shore." He glanced at Nurse Willie who sat motionless on her stool. Her dark eyes ignored the lure makings and focused unblinking on him. Brady turned back to Matt. "I called to you, but when I finally got to shore, you were gone. You left me."

Matt's head moved slowly from side to side, his wide eyes never leaving Brady's face. He spoke barely above a whisper.

"I wasn't out there last night. I was here at camp, in the chapel, begging God to keep you safe."

The hair on Brady's neck stood up. He managed to swallow, forcing the dry lump down his throat. "Then who was out there calling to me last night?"

CHAPTER 17

"I don't know who called you, but it wasn't me." Matt dropped into the chair, pulled it closer and leaned forward. "You almost gave up? Why?"

"Why not?" Brady wrapped his arms around his knees. "If I didn't make it to shore, I figured I'd get hit by lightning. Mom doesn't want me. Dad doesn't want me." He pulled his knees tighter to his chest and sighed. "I was reaching to undo my lifejacket when I heard you call."

Matt shook his head. "Wasn't me. Wish I could say it was, but I'm not your hero."

Brady was insistent. "Who else would be out there calling my name in a storm?"

"God." Willie's whisper startled him. Her normally rough voice held such confidence and awe, both he and Matt looked at her. His arms prickled with goose bumps.

Willie's dark eyes held him spellbound. "The Lord called

169

your name. Storms don't bother Him. He made 'em! And your Heavenly Father loves you more than any earthly parents ever will. Just because you don't know He's there doesn't mean He isn't. God never abandons his children." Her voice grew louder, more adamant.

Brady's arms fell away from his knees and he sat up straight. His eyes cut toward Matt as he tried to absorb Willie's words. God called his name? For real? He looked back to Willie.

"Zeke talked about recognizing God's voice. But how am I supposed to know it's God if He sounds like someone else?"

She rolled her stool closer to him and spoke softly. "God speaks in many different ways: through scripture, dreams, prayer, circumstances. Maybe this time, you needed a voice you'd recognize. How many times did you hear it?"

Brady's shoulders lifted. "A bunch." His gaze skipped between Willie and Matt. "Every time I wanted to quit, I'd hear my name. Why would God do that?"

"Because He's in the business of saving people." Willie rolled her stool back, slapped her palm on the counter and picked up her lures, as if that explained everything.

Brady shivered, but the goose bumps were replaced by warmth as if a blanket were being wrapped around him. "He's real, isn't He? It's like Zeke said, I knew about God but I never really knew Him. Until now, He was just a story to me."

The lures on Willie's hat tinkled as she nodded in agreement.

Matt grinned, his eyes reflecting the same amazement Brady felt. He clamped Brady's hand in his and held it up. "Yeah, He's real, all right. And now you know how much He loves you. When your parents or your friends let you down, when we aren't there for you, remember what happened last night."

Matt's words flowed from Brady's head down to his heart. "Will He ever talk to me again?"

Willie made a couple quick snips on a nylon fishing line. "Oh, He'll talk, but not always in the same way. Sometimes it depends on you."

"Me?" Brady frowned. "Do I have to be in trouble again, like last night?"

She swiveled her stool to face him. "Not necessarily, but you do have to listen. The police and others were out all night looking for you, calling your name. You never heard them. Maybe you couldn't hear them in the boathouse. Maybe the storm was too loud, or you were asleep. Sometimes, life's noisy storms can drown out the Lord's voice. That doesn't mean He's not speaking to you. Just means you have to listen harder. Pretty soon, you'll recognize His voice even in the middle of a storm." She held up a finished lure. "But He won't always sound like Matt."

Willie's comments rolled around in Brady's mind. He looked at Matt, lips curling into a sly grin.

"Hey, since you talk like God, the next time I get dumped in the lake, think you could walk on water to rescue me?"

Silence. Willie and Matt both stared at him then turned to look at each other. Willie giggled and bent over her lures while Matt threw his head back and laughed.

"I think the storm must've knocked you silly. That's the first joke I've heard out of you all week." Matt gathered up the breakfast tray and got to his feet. "I need to get these back to the kitchen and hustle over to morning worship. How long do you have to stay here?"

Brady looked to Willie.

"He checks out fine, but I can't release him without

Zeke's okay."

Matt reached out for a fist bump. "Glad you're back safe. Have you talked to your mom?"

Brady's smile flattened, and he gathered his knees to his chest again. "Zeke let me call her on the way back to camp, but she didn't answer."

Matt looked down, lips pressed together. Releasing a deep breath, he raised his head. "Well then, we'll keep praying for her. See ya later."

Willie tied a knot in the fishing line. "Why don't you lie down and rest until Zeke comes back?"

Brady lay down, stretching out his tight muscles before relaxing them. He plumped the pillow under his head, inhaling the fresh, clean smell of the pillowcase.

Knowing God was real made him feel different inside. He'd gone to church and learned the stories from the Bible when he was little, but God always seemed more like an old grandfather who lived a long way away. When Mom stopped going to church after Dad left, it kind of felt like God left too. The Bible stories had about as much meaning as the sinking of the Titanic. No doubt it happened, but it really didn't affect him.

Zeke talked about God in a different way, calling it a relationship. Probably something like his friendship with Steven or Matt. But how can you be friends with someone who's invisible? He'd never heard God say anything, until last night.

Brady turned on his side, facing the wall, and closed his eyes. He replayed of the voice from the storm, calling to him. *Brady. Brady.* He dreamed he was out on the water again, paddling in the dark, but not getting anywhere. There was the voice. Only this time, it sounded like Mom.

"Brady?"

Someone rubbed his back. He opened his eyes and tried to separate dream from reality. Twisting his neck around, he saw Zeke and Nurse Willie talking, their heads bent close together.

"Brady."

That *is* Mom's voice. It wasn't a dream. He rolled all the way over and found her sitting on the bed next to him. She must have just gotten there because she still wore sunglasses.

"What are you doing here?" He didn't mean it to sound unwelcoming. "I thought you weren't coming."

"When Zeke called and said you were missing, I had to come."

"What about Richard?"

Mom bit her lower lip. "He doesn't know I left." She inhaled and let it out slowly. "Well, he might know by now, but he was . . . sleeping . . . when I left." Her eyes softened as she reached out to touch his hair. "I'm so glad you're safe."

Brady sat up and tried to sort out his conflicting feelings toward her. Five days ago, she'd rejected him, said she didn't want him anymore. Now she acted like the familiar Mom he knew and trusted. But could he trust her? He couldn't see her eyes behind the sunglasses.

Funny, he was so used to seeing Steven in dark glasses, he hadn't really thought about Mom still wearing hers inside.

"Don't you want to take your glasses off?"

She lowered her head, hands clutching the sunglasses to keep them in place. The bottom edge of her sleeve moved just enough to reveal a sliver of blue- black bruise on her upper arm.

"Did he hurt you?" Brady took her arm and pushed the sleeve back. His pulse rose. "He hit you, didn't he?"

Zeke and Willie fell silent as Mom's hands dropped away

from the glasses and moved to cup her quivering chin. She bit her lower lip again and she nodded.

"Let me see." Brady took hold of her wrists and demanded again. "Let me see. I knew something was happening when I called yesterday. Your voice didn't sound right. That's why I ran away, Mom. I was trying to get home and help. What did he do to you?"

Mom kept her eyes averted while she pulled one hand from Brady's grasp and slid the glasses down her nose. Her left eye was swollen half-shut. The skin around it blazed an angry red.

Willie's shoes made no sound as she moved to inspect the eye. She reached to take Mom's hand and put an arm around her shoulders. Mom leaned into Willie's embrace, tears squeezing out from the swollen eye as her sobs broke the silence. Willie nodded to Zeke, who pulled out his cell phone and started punching in numbers as he retreated outdoors.

Brady's breath came fast and heavy. His own mother abandoned him to stay with a man who beat her. He ground out one word through clenched teeth.

"Why?"

Mom swallowed and swiped at her tears. "He didn't want me to come. I think he's jealous of you."

"That's not what I mean. You sent me away so you could stay with him. Why? How could you do that?" Brady's eyes narrowed. "Your own son!"

Mom flinched, and Willie's rebuke was swift.

"Here, now. No need to talk like that when your mama's hurting."

Mom held up her hand. "He's right." She pushed herself upright, squeezed Willie's hand before letting it go, and laid her sunglasses on the bed. After wiping her sniffles and taking several deep breaths, she spoke.

"I sent you away to protect you." Her chin trembled. "I didn't see Richard's drinking problem until after we married. He kept it hidden. I asked him not to drink while you were around and he agreed. But one night, when you stayed over at Tony's, he came home drunk and started calling me names and shoving me around." Her voice broke. Willie handed her a tissue.

The memory of that night flashed through his mind. Or rather, the memory of the next day. He'd come home from his friend's house, expecting to go to the car show with Richard. Instead, Mom said he was sick and needed to sleep. He did look sick when he woke up, and Brady expected her to pamper Richard, the way she treated him whenever he was too sick to go to school. Instead, she kept her distance, and never once asked if she could get something to make him feel better.

Mom blew her nose and reached out to touch Brady's knee. "He promised it wouldn't happen again, but it got worse. I was afraid he'd start in on you." Her fingers tightened. "I didn't choose him over you. I only wanted to protect you."

Her words flowed over and through Brady. Tension seeped away. His fists opened and he sat back on his ankles until another question demanded an answer.

"But why didn't you leave? Why stay around and let him beat you up?" His voice held its harsh tone. Mom's shoulders hunched, and she took a shuddering breath. She'd never looked so small and defenseless.

"I thought maybe I could help him if I stayed. I didn't want another divorce. For you or for me." She shook her head then reached for his hands, taking both of them in hers. Her eyes sought his and held them. "Leaving you here was the hardest thing I've ever done. Your father isn't much of a dad, but I knew he'd never hit you. I'd never send you away for any other reason."

Brady pulled his hands away. Willie scowled like she wasn't happy with his attitude as she turned back to her desk and pulled items from the cupboards. But the anger he'd nursed about his family's situation wasn't going to disappear in an instant.

Mom eased from the bed to the chair. She bent forward to rest her elbows on her knees and dropped her head, covering her face with her hands. "I'm so sorry, Brady. I've made such a mess of our lives."

He pulled his stiff legs out from under him and stretched. For some reason, the word forgiveness stuck in his mind. Was he supposed to forgive her? First Taylor, now Mom.

He slid from the bed until his feet were on the floor, his knees touching Mom's. Taking her wrists again, he pressed her hands open and held them in his.

"Mom." He waited for her to lift her head and look at him. "I forgive you."

Tears poured down her cheeks like last night's rain. He didn't know what he expected, but this wasn't it. He blinked, pulled back and let go of her hands. What should he do? He hated seeing her cry; it scared him. He looked to Willie whose hat tinkled as she nodded her approval.

"Here, put this on your mama's eye," she said.

He took the cold pack and held it out to his mom. She wiped her eyes and nose before gingerly placing it against her upper cheek and eye. He had one more question for her, though he was afraid of what her answer might be.

"Are you going back...to him?"

Her good eye closed, and she inhaled, holding it a moment before letting it out slowly. "I don't know. Probably not right away. I need some time to think." She opened her eye and looked directly at him. "But whatever I do, I'm not leaving you behind. Never again."

CHAPTER 18

The chapel's stage was decked out for the talent show with blue and white banners hanging from the ceiling. Matching streamers decorated the walls and the piano. A large projection screen provided a plain backdrop for the talent show acts.

Sitting next to Steven in the second row, Brady whispered a brief description of the dance routine accompanying Claire's and Hayley's song. His eyes never left the stage, taking full advantage of the chance to watch Claire's every move.

Steven elbowed him. "You like her, don't you?"

His gaze swung from the stage to Steven. "Who?"

"Claire. You were grinning just now when you told me what she was doing."

Brady pressed his lips together, trying to keep the corners from turning up. "How would you know whether I'm grinning or not?"

"I can hear it in the way you talk." Steven sat up straight, a smug smile on his face. "Don't worry. It's cool."

Amazing. They hadn't known each other for a full week, and now Steven, who couldn't see a thing, was reading him better than his friends back home ever did— kids who'd known him for years. Brady's cheeks burned remembering how he'd lied to him. Steven forgave him after he explained why he left and what Mom looked like when she got here this morning. Not only forgave him, but agreed he'd done the right thing. Steven even said he would've covered for him if he'd known the reason.

The girls finished their performance and Claire flung herself into the seat next to Brady, breathing hard. "Whew! Glad that's over."

"You were great." His knee was warm against hers, and it wasn't just the temperature in the crowded chapel.

"Thanks!" She smiled, complete with dimples, and ran her fingers through her bangs, holding them back while her other hand fanned her face.

As the announcer brought up the next act, he glanced over at his mom. A large bandage hid her bruised eye better than sunglasses. His jaw tightened. Imagining the scene at home last night nearly gave him the heaves. His blood grew hot at the thought.

Leaving Mom in the clinic when he was released wasn't easy, but Zeke and Willie promised to settle her in a guest room where she could rest. He'd visited her this afternoon, and was relieved to learn that Zeke persuaded her not to return to Richard until they'd both attended counseling. So they wouldn't go home tomorrow, but the rest of their plans were like the balls being juggled onstage. They might end up staying in the guesthouse until Monday when Mom had to go back to work.

Claire nudged him when the announcer called his name. His stomach did a somersault. He shouldn't have eaten so much carrot cake at supper. The familiar butterflies rumbled more like cargo planes under all that frosting. He climbed the steps and stood center stage. Mom smiled and gestured with two thumbs pointing to the ceiling. From the corner of his eye, he saw Claire pump her fist, but he didn't dare look at her.

He inhaled deeply, slowly, willing himself to relax. Moistening his lips, he raised the horn to his mouth and the melody of "Amazing Grace" soared through the room crisp and clear. His eyes found the back corner of the ceiling where he was safe from distraction. He played the first verse at a soft, easy pace then bumped it up to a march tempo the second time through. The third verse was a jazz version and the audience responded by clapping along. The tempting rhythm even had him tapping his toe.

Finally, he slowed it down, his breath traveling from the mouthpiece through the valves beneath his fingers and out into the chapel on reverent notes. The words of the sacred song flowed through his mind. He was lost, but now was found. He'd been blind to God's love for him – as unseeing as Steven. Now he saw clearly how God wanted to be part of his life every day. The words pressed on his heart. Through many dangers, toils and snares, God's grace had kept him safe so far, and grace would lead him home.

***

Zeke dismissed the campers for a quick break before campfire, and invited the parents to the dining hall for coffee and refreshments. Claire left with her friends, and Brady ran back to the cabin to drop off his trumpet. He returned to find Mom waiting with Steven.

"I just wanted to say goodnight." She hugged him close

and gave him a quick kiss on the cheek.

He should've been embarrassed, but not tonight. He returned the hug and said goodnight, then took Steven to the Snack Shack for a bag of corn chips before they made their way down to the campfire. He'd gotten used to the depth of darkness out here, but when Steven tripped over something, he missed his flashlight. It sure didn't do him any good on the bottom of the lake.

The logs around the campfire pit were all occupied by the time they got there, so he and Steven wiggled in among some kids sitting on the grass close to the fire. Wood-scented smoke rose, drifting in random directions and mingling with the pungent odor of mosquito repellent.

"Don't breathe," he warned Steven when the smoke turned their way. Pinching his nose as it engulfed them, he squeezed his eyes shut against the sting and fanned away the smoke. His face and arms absorbed the toasty warmth from the campfire. The smoke shifted directions again, and the fire's flames bobbing and dipping among the logs mesmerized him. Moisture from last night's rain escaped in a slow hiss. Behind him, the night's cool air sent a chill up his back.

Two counselors strummed guitars to start the singing, and he joined in the now-familiar melodies. These weren't the kind of songs he remembered singing in church. He'd have to persuade Mom to start going to church again. Maybe things had changed.

When the singing ended, Matt stood with a Bible in one hand, a flashlight in the other. "It's our last night together. Tomorrow, you'll all go home—back to your family, your neighborhood, your friends. What are you taking home with you besides good memories? Will life be different because of your week here at Rustic Knoll?"

Steven nudged him, offering his bag of corn chips. Brady dug his hand into the bag and pulled out a few chips, popping them into his mouth while Matt continued.

"This week, we've encouraged you to meet God in a personal way. You've heard from His own word how much He loves you. Here at camp, it's easy to believe that. But back home, you'll be challenged by people who think faith in God is ridiculous. Some kids will laugh at you. A teacher might make fun of you. Maybe the guy or girl you really want to impress will say you're stupid to believe in God. Then what?"

Matt aimed the flashlight beam at the Bible's pages. "Listen to this. 'You will know the truth and the truth will set you free.' When you've studied for a math test and you know the answers, you're not all tied up with worry and fear. You're free!

"Tonight, I'm asking you to decide. Will you believe the truth?" He raised the Bible over his head. "Or will you believe the lies the world tells you? If you feel worthless, if you think God can't love you after what you've done, those are lies. Let the truth of God's love set you free."

Sparks from the fire danced high into the air before blinking out. Brady had believed a lot of lies this week, lies that kept him tied up in knots. Six days ago, he believed Mom wanted to get rid of him because she cared for Richard more than him. Wrong! He'd assumed camp would be awful and boring. Wrong again. He'd thought God didn't exist, or if He did, He didn't care enough to notice him. Seriously wrong!

The truth was Mom loved him enough to protect him, even when it meant she'd get hurt. Camp was a lot of fun; he'd made some good friends here. As for God, He was definitely real and He cared.

Right now, he may not have an address, but God knew

where he was. Even in the middle of a lake, in the dark of night and the fury of a thunderstorm, God saw him and took care of him. Yeah, he believed. No, he *knew* God would guide them home as surely as He'd guided Brady to shore.

***

Saturday morning passed in a frenzied, sleep–deprived blur. If he'd known the chores required before they could leave, he might not have stayed awake half the night. After breakfast, they'd packed and dragged all their stuff outside before vacuuming, scrubbing toilets and sinks and wiping down the shower stalls. All that remained now was to say good-bye.

With mixed feelings, he tied his duffle bag to Steven's suitcase handle. It hadn't been an easy week. Parts of it had been no fun at all, but if he didn't come back next summer he might never see Steven or Claire again. He shrugged his backpack on and picked up his sleeping bag, pillow and trumpet. Steven pulled the suitcase and they headed toward the main building to meet Mrs. Miller. She greeted both of them with a hug.

"I hope Steven behaved himself this week and didn't get you into any trouble." A wink accompanied her teasing tone, but Steven objected.

"Me? I wasn't the one who got in trouble."

Mrs. Miller raised an eyebrow. "Oh? Does that mean someone else did?"

Brady elbowed him, and Steven hesitated only a moment. "Yeah, one guy in our cabin was a jerk. He landed in Zeke's office a couple times."

Brady released the breath he'd been holding as Matt jogged up, catching Mrs. Miller's attention with a hand on her shoulder.

"Hey! It was great having Steven in my cabin this week. You must be very proud of him."

Mrs. Miller beamed and thanked him. Matt clasped Steven's hand, pulling him into a man-hug, then did the same with Brady. "You guys keep in touch, okay? I won't be online much until school starts again but don't forget about me. I want to hear what's going on."

He winked and gave Brady a fist bump. "Let me know how everything works out."

"I will."

Matt jogged off toward Zeke's office. Brady untied his bag from Steven's suitcase.

Mrs. Miller took her son's sleeping bag and pillow. "I hope you'll be back next year, Brady. I know Steven will be anxious to hang out with you again."

"Yeah, call me sometime, okay?" Steven took his mom's arm and they started toward the parking lot.

"Okay," Brady called. "See you next year."

A steady stream of campers and parents laden with luggage trudged toward the parking lot now. Dillon waved to him from the crowd and shouted.

"Next year, you're on my team!"

Brady grinned and waved back. Keeping an eye out for Claire, he wrapped the duffle bag's strap around one hand and dragged it behind him. Halfway to his mom's room, he spotted Claire. She saw him, too, and left her parents to run over to him.

"I hoped we'd get to say good-bye." Her arms encircled a pillow and a worn pink teddy bear. With one hand, she pulled a phone from her back pocket. "Can I get a picture of us?"

"Sure." He set down his trumpet case and his pulse quickened as she stepped close, bending her head next to his.

His nostrils tingled at her fresh, clean scent.

"Smile," she said, holding the phone in front of them. Click. She checked the picture—a close-up of their faces that would look awesome on his mirror at home. "Perfect."

"I want that too."

"I'll send it to you. Look me up online as soon as you get home." She threw an arm around his neck and squeezed. "Take care, Brady. And come back next year!" With that, she ran to catch up with her parents.

He stared after her, trying to capture everything about her to savor once he got home. Wherever that might be. Mom met him at the guesthouse door, keys in hand.

"You ready?" She looked better today, wearing her dark sunglasses again.

"We're leaving? Where are we going?"

She singled out the car key, the rest of the keys jingling below her palm. "To your dad's. I talked to him last night."

Brady's knees went weak. After all that had happened, surely she wouldn't send him away again. "I'm not living with him, am I?"

"Yes, but..."

"Mo-om! You said..."

Mom held her hand up at his protest. "Let me explain. I called to let him know he didn't need to drive up for you today. When he heard everything that had happened, he said we could stay at his place. He'll be out of town for the next couple weeks anyway, so we'll have it to ourselves."

"He was planning to leave me alone for two weeks?" Brady shook his head and scuffed his foot against the ground. Dad hadn't changed. Business always came first.

Mom hoisted his duffle bag onto her hip. "He's not a bad person, honey. Just clueless when it comes to relationships."

She started for the parking lot.

Weird. The father he could see and touch took no interest in his life and thought nothing of leaving him alone for two weeks. His heavenly Father, who couldn't be seen or touched, knew every detail of his life and was always there for him.

"Brady?" Mom called. "Come on, let's go. I want to hear about your week."

His arm tightened around the pillow and sleeping bag, and he hurried to catch up. He'd probably still be talking about his week when they reached Dad's house.

THANK YOU

If you enjoyed this novel, please consider leaving the author a review. Your thoughts and feedback are very much appreciated.

RESOURCES

Abuse: If you or someone you know is hurt by verbal or physical abuse, it's important to talk to someone you trust. This could be a pastor, school counselor, a trusted teacher, friend's parent, or a neighbor. Abuse is NOT your fault, so don't be embarrassed about it.

Alcoholism: Alcoholics Anonymous runs a program for families of those addicted to alcohol. Go to http://al-anon.alateen.org/ to find a group in your area.

Divorce: Divorce Care for Kids (www.DC4K.org) is a support program to help kids deal with their parents' divorce. www.divorceandteens.weebly.com

Running Away: For help before or after you decide to run away from home, try www.1800runaway.org
If you need to find a safe place, try www.nationalsafeplace.org

Christian camps: To find a camp in your area, type "Christian Youth Camps" and your state into any search engine. Or go to the Christian Camp and Conference Association: www.ccca.org

QUESTIONS FOR FURTHER THOUGHT

1. Brady is stunned by his mother's announcement that he must now live with his dad. How did his reaction affect his mom's response? How might he have handled it better?

2. Taylor enjoyed teasing Brady. How did Brady's reaction give Taylor a sense of power? Near the end, when Brady sees his friends in the clinic, he realizes jealousy over his friendship with Claire might have motivated Taylor's teasing. What are some other reasons kids tease and bully?

3. Steven was used to kids making fun of him and had learned not to let it bother him. Right from the start, he defended Brady from Taylor's criticism, even if it meant he would become a target as well. How else could you help someone who is being teased or bullied?

4. Brady observes two ways of dealing with conflict. Steven urges him to ignore it and walk away. Claire faces it head on. Which way do you think is better? Are there situations where one might be a better choice than the other?

5. Have you ever been bullied or had kids make fun of you? How did you handle it? Think of as many different ways as possible to manage bullies.

6. Zeke pointed out the difference between knowing about someone and knowing him or her personally. Brady realized he only knew about God. What steps should he take to develop a personal relationship with God?

7. Forgiveness is a difficult thing to do when we don't think the other person deserves it. What reasoning did Matt use to show Brady he could forgive Taylor even if he didn't want to? How did Brady learn to forgive Taylor?

8. In his blackest moment, Brady was ready to give up on life. What lie did he believe that made him give up hope? What truth did he learn when he got back to camp?

9. Nurse Willie tells Brady that God speaks in many different ways. Name some of the ways we can hear from God. How should Brady train himself to recognize God's voice?

10. Brady's mom kept her troubles to herself, which meant Brady couldn't understand her decision to send him to his dad. Even though it wasn't his fault, it affected his life in a huge way. How might this story help kids when adults in their life take action that seems unreasonable?

ACKNOWLEDGEMENTS

So many people have taken part in the writing of this book. Their names should be on the cover along with mine. My critique groups especially deserve my undying gratitude for helping to shape and polish this story: the West Houston Meetup group, and the ACFW YA critique group.

For their constant support and encouragement, I thank my writing friends Tanya Eavenson, Deb Garland, Kelli Hughett, Terri Wangard and Peggy Wirgau. You girls believed in my story when I had given up hope. Special thanks to Donna Watson, Kendyl Woods, Meredith McWhirter and the others who read the finished manuscript and gave me valuable feedback. Your time and consideration is most appreciated.

To the Kingsland Book Club ladies—Phillis, Jackie, Diana, Leslee and Mary—I learned a lot about writing from our book discussions. I promise I won't write you into my books without your permission.

My children—Daniel, Beki and Matt—and my dear husband Wayne always encouraged and cheered me on. I love you all deeply.

My late parents, Rev. Paul and Florence Watson, provided our family with the unique experience of growing up at a camp. Carol, Paul and Donna, Barb, David, Ernie and Karen, I hope this book stirs up as many fond memories for you as it did for me.

Most importantly, I give all the glory to my Lord Jesus Christ. Any criticism of this book belongs to me, but all praise belongs to Him who alone is worthy.

ABOUT THE AUTHOR

Mary L. Hamilton grew up at a camp in southern Wisconsin much like the setting for her Rustic Knoll novels. Her experiences during twenty years of living at the camp, as well as people she knew there, inspired many of the events and situations in her novels.

When not writing, Mary enjoys reading, needlecrafts, being outdoors and spending time with her family. She and her husband make their home in Texas.

Connect with Mary:
    www.MaryHamiltonBooks.com
    www.Facebook.com/MaryHamiltonBooks
    www.Pinterest.com/mhamiltonbooks

KEEP READING FOR A
SNEAK PEAK AT

SPEAK NO EVIL

RUSTIC KNOLL BIBLE CAMP
BOOK TWO

CHAPTER 1

Taylor Dixon riveted his gaze to the red Corvette pulling into the parking lot of Rustic Knoll Bible Camp. Its supercharged engine purred like a monster cat as the 'Vette prowled the rows of parked cars hunting a space of its own, finally settling across two slots in the back row.

Forgetting Dad's command to unload the car, Taylor stuffed his auto magazine into his pillow and put some distance between himself and the family's van. He drank in the Corvette's sleek body, his heart racing with the engine as the driver revved it up before shutting off the machine. Oh, for a closer look, but he didn't dare. Not with Dad nearby. His younger sister came up and leaned into him.

"Nice." Marissa drew the word out, keeping her voice low.

"It's awesome."

Her finger poked his side. "I wasn't talking about the car."

Taylor glanced sideways at her, then looked back at the 'Vette.

A boy about Taylor's age emerged from the passenger's seat. The kid stretched and surveyed the parking lot, a smug grin hugging his face. His eyes met Taylor's. One eyebrow arched as he lifted his chin high. His grin changed to a smirk before his gaze slid over to Marissa.

Wait. Was that a wink?

Marissa stiffened, caught her breath and stifled a squeal. She squeezed Taylor's arm, her fingernails biting into the soft skin of his inner elbow. But before he had time to consider some guy flirting with his sister, Dad finger-thumped his head.

"Don't get any ideas. You're not getting your driver's license. I don't want you anywhere near a car like that until you're eighteen and I'm not responsible for you anymore."

Taylor huffed and turned back to their drab gray minivan. "Dad, I'm at camp, remember? Swimming? Softball? Sermons? No cars."

"Yeah, so quit drooling and get your stuff out of the car. I don't want to be here all day."

Ducking under the liftback, Taylor muttered while he pulled out his duffle and sleeping bag. "I wasn't drooling."

Reaching for her pillow, Marissa giggled and whispered, "I was."

Taylor growled. "Forget it, Riss. He's a stuck-up snob."

"How do you know? You haven't even met him." She didn't bother to keep her voice down.

"Didn't you see the way he looked down his nose at us? He thinks he's hot because he came to camp in a 'Vette."

"Oh, he's hot even without the car. Maybe he looked down his nose at you, but he winked at me. Admit it. You saw it, too." Marissa struggled to pull her suitcase out of the van.

"Ugh! Can you get that out for me?"

Taylor tugged on her overstuffed bag. "What's in here? You must've packed your whole bedroom." He hauled it out and set it on the ground.

"Everybody ready?" Mom grabbed her purse and closed the passenger door.

Dad shut the liftback door. Even though it was summer, he wore his football coach's shirt. Dad's hefty build and graying buzz-cut hair were so different from Taylor's, few kids at school ever guessed he was Coach Dixon's son. Before Taylor took two steps with his own duffle bag on wheels, Dad clamped a vise grip on his shoulder. "Take your sister's suitcase. It's too heavy for her."

Taylor handed Marissa his pillow and sleeping bag, then dragged both their suitcases across the gravel parking lot. Marissa's had to be loaded with bricks. He stopped to switch hands. "Riss, we're only here for a week. Why'd you bring so much stuff?"

"I only brought what I need." Marissa repositioned her purse strap on her shoulder, then shifted the pillows to her other arm. "Taybo, I can't wait until you have a car like that Corvette."

Dad grunted. "In his dreams."

"His dreams will come true. One day, he'll be a famous race car driver and he'll get to drive Mustangs and Corvettes and all kinds of hot cars." She threw a smile Taylor's way. "And he'll take his favorite sister for a ride in them, too. Won't you?"

Dad shot Taylor a warning look. "He'll stay miles away from those cars if he knows what's good for him."

Arguing was useless, but Taylor couldn't help it. "Can't I at least get my license? I'm almost sixteen. All my friends are

197

learning to drive, and I pulled my grades up like you wanted."

"Prove to me you deserve to drive." Dad might as well have been talking to one of his players.

"How? What do I have to do?"

"Show me you're responsible by staying out of trouble."

Like that would ever happen. Not as long as he kept getting blamed for Marissa's adventures. Taylor gave up, but Marissa continued the argument.

"Daddy, just because Jesse stole a car and went to jail doesn't mean Taylor will, too."

"Princess, you can stick up for your brother all you want, but I know boys. Taylor hung around Jesse and those delinquent friends of his. Who knows what they taught him?"

Mom threw a glance at them over her shoulder. "Can we not talk about this right now?"

Taylor slowed, letting the others walk ahead of him. Marissa was only thirteen but the way things were going, she'd get her license before he did. The family princess. And Jesse was the prince, Dad's favorite from the moment he put on a football uniform.

Where does that leave me? Stuck between a princess and a prince.

Taylor yanked hard on Marissa's suitcase and joined the rest of his family at the end of the check-in line. Nurse Willie manned the registration table like last year, wearing her weird hat with the fishing lures all over it. He'd almost persuaded Mom to let him stay home this summer. But then Marissa decided camp sounded like fun, and if she was going, he had to go, too.

Taylor searched the line for a familiar face, but didn't recognize anyone from last year. Whenever they inched forward, Dad checked his watch and sighed loud enough for everyone nearby to hear.

Marissa nudged Taylor's arm. "Tell me what the buildings are so I don't get lost. That one must be the church." She pointed to the chapel with its steep roof and blue cross-shaped window.

Taylor nodded toward the nearest low building with redwood stained siding. "That's the dining hall. The girls' cabins are over on the other side of it. Guys cabins are over this way, past the chapel."

"What's that little hut over there?" Marissa indicated the small building at one end of the dining hall.

"That's the Snack Shack. A message board is posted on the outside wall on the other side. You'll need to look there for your Rec team assignment and daily activities."

"Will we be on the same rec team?"

"I hope not. You're such a klutz, we'd never win anything."

"Hey!" Marissa punched his arm and turned her back to him, acting insulted.

But it was true. Marissa was as uncoordinated as Jesse was athletic.

Jesse. Even though five years separated them, Jesse had always let him tag along, announcing to his friends, "Hey everybody! Taylor's here. Say hi to my little brother." Had there really been a note of pride in Jesse's voice or was it his imagination, wishful thinking on his part? For a while, he'd taken on his brother's shuffling walk and the way he pointed both thumbs in the air when something pleased him. But Jesse had often teased him, too, and they'd had their fights. Still, when Jesse was around to toss a football or shoot hoops, it was easier to handle the lack of attention from Dad. Hopefully prison wouldn't change his brother too much by the time he got out.

When they finally reached the check-in table set up in the shade of a large oak tree, Mom handed their health forms to Nurse Willie.

Marissa eyed Willie, her white hair a contrast with her dark skin, and the bucket hat adorned with fishing lures atop her head. "Cool hat."

Dad rolled his eyes and walked away, shaking his head.

"Thank you." Willie scanned their health forms. "You must be Taylor's sister. Good to see you again, Taylor. Looks like you've grown a couple inches since last year." She held the papers out so the counselor sitting next to her could see the names. "Lauren, this is Taylor Dixon and his sister, Marissa. Taylor was here last year."

"Hi! Welcome to Rustic Knoll." Lauren's smile showed off perfectly white teeth. A bit of red chewing gum peeked from the corner of her mouth. "Marissa and Taylor?" She snapped her gum and slid her finger down a list of names. After highlighting two in pink, she looked up. "Okay, Marissa, you are in Magnolia Cabin. That's back over here." She pointed to the right behind her back. "And Taylor, you're in Spruce Cabin."

"I know where it is." Taylor let go of Marissa's suitcase and flexed his hand a few times. No way was he dragging that thing to the cabin for her. He glanced again down the check-in line for a familiar face. He knew the kid with red hair who was standing with the one wearing dark glasses.

Brady and Steven were in his cabin last year, but he didn't expect a friendly greeting from them. Not after all the trouble he gave them. The girl with short blonde hair talking with Brady and Steven was Claire Thompson. No surprise there. She and Steven and Brady were buddies. Would Claire remember him? Taylor caught her eye and waved, but she barely lifted a hand before turning away. Not the response he'd hoped for.

"Who's that? She's cute!" Marissa sounded incredulous, as if surprised he would know any pretty girls.

"Yeah, but she didn't look too impressed," Dad said. "I'd say she's a little out of your league." He prodded Taylor away from the check-in table. "Show me to your cabin, Hot Shot."

"Aren't you going to help Marissa with her suitcase?" Anything to keep Dad from accompanying him to the cabin. Mom moved the suitcase away from the check-in table. "We girls can manage." She kissed Taylor's cheek, and gave him a quick hug. "Bye, Honey. Have a good week. We'll see you on Saturday." Mom took hold of the suitcase handle. "C'mon, Marissa."

Dad urged Taylor forward. "Let's go."

Taylor yanked his bag behind him, using his chin-length brown hair to cover the frown on his face. Last year, Mom brought him to camp while Dad stayed home with Marissa. But with both he and Riss coming to camp this year, Mom talked Dad into joining them for a "family outing." At least with Marissa here, he wouldn't have to endure Mom making his bed and hanging up his clothes like last year. But he could only hope no one else was in the cabin to hear Dad's opinions.

They skirted the chapel, walking alongside the windows that looked out over the lake. Dad peered inside. "How often do they make you go to church here?"

"All morning, plus another worship session in the evening."

"Worship session? You mean like Sunday church?"

Taylor shrugged. "Kinda, but the music's more like our kind of music." His roller bag bounced and tipped when they reached the end of the sidewalk.

"You listen to what the preacher says?"

"Sometimes." Taylor righted the bag and tugged on it. The wheels didn't work so well in the grass.

"Sometimes? If you want your license, you'd better pay attention all the time, y'hear? Your mother and I don't need another jailbird, like your no-good brother." Dad whacked the back of Taylor's head. Not hard, but his wedding ring bit into Taylor's skull.

"Ow!" Taylor dropped his sleeping bag and rubbed his head. "I'm not Jesse. Okay?"

"We'll see. You listen to that preacher every time he talks. Do you understand?"

"Okay!" Taylor moved out of ring-shot range. Nothing he did would ever convince Dad he wasn't running in Jesse's footsteps. His brother, the star player on the school's football team, could do no wrong. But he'd fooled everyone, including Dad whose dreams of borrowed glory got smashed when Jesse quit the team, got arrested and sent to prison.

They skirted the giant blue spruce tree that identified the cabin and Taylor climbed the two concrete steps to the front door. The screen door squeaked as they entered and Taylor led the way through the common room, its worn couches and ragged armchairs perfect for teenage boys to lounge on.

Dad wasted no time finding fault. "Rustic Knoll, huh? Rusty nail is more like it. And we pay good money for this."

Taylor entered the bunkroom and tossed his sleeping bag onto the first empty bed, shoving his duffle bag underneath. A couple of sleeping bags lay tossed on other bunks, but the cabin was empty at the moment. Now, if he could get rid of Dad before anyone else arrived. He dug his hands into his pockets.

"This is it. Not much to it."

The screen door squeaked open and slammed shut. A young man with dark skin and close cut hair unlocked the door to the counselor's room before glancing in their direction. He strode toward them and extended his hand.

"Hi! I'm Harris Franks, your counselor. And you are—?"

"Taylor Dixon." He shook the counselor's hand, then watched as Harris shook Dad's hand. Dad liked to test the strength of guys' handshakes. Taylor didn't see the customary wince, but considering those biceps, he wasn't surprised. When did a counselor get time to work out?

Dad released Harris's hand. "You're here all summer? How much they pay you to live in this dump?"

Harris's brows popped up and an uncertain smile pulled at the corners of his mouth. His gaze flicked from Dad to Taylor and back to Dad. Taylor hung his head, his long bangs falling over his face.

Harris tapped his keys against his thigh. "I don't do it for the money."

"Uh-huh. You in college?" Dad eyed Harris who stood half a head taller but only half as wide. "Yes, sir."

"What's your major?"

"I'm in a Biblical Studies program, planning to enter the ministry."

"Gonna be a pastor?" Dad grunted. "Good for you. Maybe some of it'll rub off on Taylor this week. Keep your eye on him. He likes to get into trouble."

Taylor peeked at Harris through strands of brown hair.

"Don't worry, Mr. Dixon. I'm sure Taylor and I will get along fine." Harris stepped between them and gently guided Dad toward the door. "If we do have any problems, how do you suggest I discipline Taylor?"

"Well now, I'm not one for smackin' kids around..."
Dad's voice trailed off as they exited the cabin.

Except for vise grips and brain thumps. But it was the
verbal smack-downs that hurt the most.

"Taylor?" Dad called from the front steps. "You keep an
eye on your sister this week."

"Yeah, I know." Having the Princess at camp with him
was going to be a royal pain.

51540520R00127

Made in the USA
San Bernardino, CA
26 July 2017